Magic in Mistletoe

JANET KOOPS

BROWN HOUSE BOOKS

Book Cover by: The Cover Collection

1st edition 2023 by: Brown House Books

ISBN (print): 979-8-9865521-6-3
ISBN (ebook): 979-8-9865521-5-6

Also by Janet Koops

Homing Instinct
Six Weeks With You
Rules of Disengagement
Family Friends
Then I Met You (2024)

For a complete list of titles, please scan the QR code or visit janetkoops.com

Chapter 1

For a woman who'd grown up at the beach, practiced outdoor yoga, and enjoyed a morning cafecito, Sadie Wexford never expected to end up living in Alaska. And not even Anchorage. No, Sadie had landed in middle-of-nowhere-Mistletoe. Even after several months, she still wasn't accustomed to it. Each day welcomed a fresh surprise, but not the good kind. Yesterday, a bear wandered through downtown. And this morning, she'd found a mouse nest in the toaster. In. The. Toaster. She'd never eat toast again.

So it was no surprise that as she made her way to work, she questioned whether she'd ever call this place home. With a heavy sigh, Sadie crunched through the snow-covered streets. Bundled beneath a heavy winter parka, large gray scarf, hat, mittens, and big, furry boots, she could pass for a Yeti. Nonetheless, she'd resigned herself to tough it out in Mistletoe and at the Snowflake Sugar Shop. "Where every bite's cooler than ice," she said aloud, mocking the store's slogan.

With her key in the lock, she paused. She should be grateful. Inheriting the store had been the only beacon of hope after many terrible months. She'd been down to her last few hundred dollars when the probate attorney called her. Initially, Sadie believed it to be a cruel prank. Inheriting not only a house but also a business from a grandmother she never knew seemed too good to be true. But the attorney had persisted, and before she knew it, Sadie was on a plane to Alaska.

That was three months ago. And the house was technically a cabin, and the business a candy store in a small, small town.

Whummph. A bunch of snow slid off the roof, landing on her head. "Stupid snow," Sadie yelled and stomped into the store. Snow hit the mat as she shook it off her head and shoulders, her grumpy demeanor louder than any words she could have uttered.

She hung up her coat and changed her boots for shoes in the back office, then surveyed the quiet shop, preparing herself for another day of work. She'd have a much better day if she didn't have to deal with customers.

The door jingled open, and a gust of cold air ushered in Rosie, the Snowflake Sugar Shop's resident candy maker. Her curly red hair bounced in time with the jingles of the door chimes.

"Good morning, Sadie." Her cheerful voice cut through the peace like a sharp sword. Her bright green eyes sparkled as she shook the snow off her coat, and her mere presence infused the store with energy.

"How?" Sadie grunted. "How are you this happy when we only have daylight for about five hours? I come to work in the dark. I go home in the dark. It's depressing." She could feel Rosie's eyes on her and braced herself for the inevitable onslaught of positivity that was sure to follow. This type of exchange had become part of their morning ritual.

"The snow," Rosie said, peering out the window. "It's a winter wonderland out there. I love it."

"That's crazy. Every snowflake is another reason to stay in bed," Sadie replied. "I miss the sand under my feet and the sun's heat on my face." She focused intently on the candy in front of her, determined not to let Rosie's cheerfulness seep into her own mood.

"Come on, Sadie. It's almost Christmas. Surely even you can find some joy in that?"

"Joy?" Sadie scoffed, rolling her eyes. "I'll find joy when I don't have to deal with biting wind, shoveling snow, and layers and layers of clothes." She finally looked up at Rosie, trying to silently convey how uninterested she was in discussing holiday cheer.

Undeterred, Rosie approached the counter. "What if," she began, her eyes twinkling with mischief, "we make a bet? If something brings you genuine holiday cheer, you have to wear a Santa hat from then until Christmas. Deal?"

Sadie eyed Rosie skeptically, considering her proposition. She knew it was highly unlikely that anything could turn her into a festive en-thusiast, so the risk was minimal. "Fine," she relented, extending her hand to seal the deal.

"Deal!" Rosie declared, giving Sadie's hand a firm shake.

The door to the Snowflake Sugar Shop jingled merrily as a group of customers stepped inside, bringing with them a rush of frosty air. Sadie forced herself not to scowl as the icy breeze penetrated her sweater, causing goosebumps to break out over her arms. She rubbed them to warm up as she turned to face the customers.

"Welcome," she said flatly.

Rosie flashed a bright smile at the newcomers from behind the counter, her green eyes sparkling with genuine friendliness. "Hi there. Let us know if you need help finding anything," she called out cheerfully, her voice carrying easily through the cozy shop. A few customers grinned in response, clearly taken in by Rosie's infectious optimism.

"Have a look around," Sadie added, though her words lacked the same enthusiasm.

"Sadie, at least try to smile," Rosie whispered, leaning in close. "These are your customers. Don't scare them away."

"I'm trying," Sadie grumbled, begrudgingly attempting to soften her expression. As the customers browsed, she watched Rosie assist them. The contrast between her and Sadie stung–while Rosie glowed with an inner light, Sadie lived under a rain cloud.

An older woman with tight gray curls approached the counter with a selection of candy-filled jars, her cheeks rosy from the cold.

"These are for my grandchildren," she explained. "They absolutely love your candy! It's such a treat during the holiday season."

"I'm glad, but that's all Rosie's doing," Sadie replied, ringing up the items, her movements stiff and efficient. "That'll be thirty-five dollars."

"You're Sadie Wexford, right? I heard you came up to take over the candy store. I'm so sorry about the loss of your grandmother. The entire community loved her."

"Thank you," Sadie replied. Since she'd never met the woman, condolences made her uncomfortable. "Here you go," she muttered, handing over the bagged candy without meeting the woman's gaze. She was not in the mood for further conversation. "Enjoy."

"Thank you so much," the customer exclaimed but remained at the counter. "I'm sure you've been told how much you look like Mable when she was your age. She had the same brown hair and ice-blue eyes, and oh, her skin was as smooth as a porcelain doll's. Exactly like yours. She was a senior when my friends and I started high school, and we thought a beauty queen had arrived in Mistletoe." The woman paused as if lost in memories. "Well, welcome to Mistletoe and Merry Christmas!"

"Happy holidays," Sadie replied, attempting to sound cheerful, but she turned away as soon as the door closed behind the woman. She stared blankly at the rows of colorful candies lining the shelves, her heart heavy with an emotion she couldn't quite place.

Sadie took a deep breath, trying to center herself amidst the chaos of the candy store. This time of year always brought out the worst in her; the forced merriment, the fake smiles, everyone pretending to be happy when she knew deep down they had their own struggles and heartaches. Why hadn't she waited until after the holidays to move to Mistletoe? Oh right, her lack of money and impending eviction.

The sound of the door chime announced the arrival of another customer, pulling Sadie out of her thoughts. She plastered on a tight-lipped approximation of a smile as a large man with a silvery beard approached the counter.

"Good afternoon," he said. "I'm hoping you can help me find the perfect assortment of candies for my grandchildren."

"Of course," Sadie replied, finding it difficult for her to share in his enthusiasm. "How many are there?"

"Eight," the man answered, holding up eight fingers with a chuckle. "They're practically bouncing off the walls with excitement for the holidays."

"Ah, yes. The 'magic' of the season," she said, air-quoting the word magic with a dismissive wave of her hand. "I'm sure their excitement is simply contagious."

"Indeed it is," the man agreed, unfazed by her sarcasm. "There's nothing quite like seeing the world alight with Christmas magic."

"Right," Sadie snorted, already gathering various candies into a bag. "That childlike wonder lasts about as long as the candy does."

"Is that what you believe?" the man asked, tilting his head as he observed her carefully.

"Experience has taught me that people rarely show their true selves," she said, setting the bag of candy on the counter. "All that holiday happiness is a facade, a mask they put on to hide their real feelings."

"Perhaps," the man conceded, paying for his purchase with a kind smile. "But sometimes, those masks can help us discover something genuine within ourselves. Something worth celebrating."

"Whatever you say," Sadie muttered, handing him his bag. "That will be forty-five dollars, please."

The man handed her cash.

"Well, Merry Christmas, I suppose," Sadie said as she put the money into the cash register.

"Thank you, my dear," the man replied, his eyes still twinkling as he turned to leave. "And a Merry Christmas to you as well. You never know what kind of magic is possible when you open your heart." He quickly double-tapped his finger on the side of his nose before pointing at her.

"That was weird," she whispered as the man exited.

Uneasy, Sadie walked over to the large window and watched the snowflakes dance slowly toward the ground. Her knees weakened, and she leaned against the window frame for support, as if unable to carry the weight of her perpetual scowl. Why had the old man unnerved her so? She didn't believe in magic or the Christmas spirit, but as the snow twinkled like a kaleidoscope under the colorful holiday lights, she secretly hoped that there existed a kernel of genuine joy waiting to be uncovered.

Chapter 2

A s Sadie finished shoveling her walkway, the winter wind whipped through the neighborhood, causing her hair to dance wildly behind her. She scanned the surrounding area with disdain.

So much snow! How did anything survive in this environment? She wasn't built for this. Not at all. But as she leaned her shovel against the wall, even beach-loving Sadie couldn't deny the cabin's rustic beauty.

If she were a creative person, she'd have taken a picture of her A-frame log cabin nestled perfectly among the snow-covered pines and sent it out as a Christmas card. But she wasn't crafty. Nor did she have anyone to send it to. Not her fault—or at least not entirely her fault.

And while the cabin was no beachfront condo, it provided her with a sense of warmth despite the harsh winter environment. With two bedrooms on the ground floor and a spacious loft overhead, it was the perfect size to endure her time in the quaint northern town.

In fact, she almost looked forward to doing the store's paperwork because she got to work from home. Even if there was a mountain of it. Running a candy store was no easy task.

"Alright, let's get inside and get to work," she said, stomping her snow-covered boots on the wooden porch before stepping inside the cabin. No sooner had Sadie removed her coat when she tripped over the area rug in the foyer. She attempted to catch herself on the coat stand, instead knocking it over. Glass shattered beside her. She whipped around and found that she'd broken the small window in the door. Pieces of broken glass lay scattered all around, glinting maliciously in the firelight as wind rushed through the cabin, blowing her carefully organized stacks of paper off the table.

"Ugh, just what I needed," she grumbled, running a hand through her hair, as if trying to tame her mounting frustration. Her eyes narrowed at the mess.

"Stupid wind," she muttered. "Stupid me." Sadie quickly searched the cabin for something to cover the hole in her door, eventually taping a piece of cardboard over the broken window. Once that was taken care of, she then fetched a broom and dustpan from the kitchen and began sweeping up the shards.

The sound of the glass tinkling against each other seemed to mock her, amplifying her irritation. Each sweep felt like it added another layer to her souring mood. As she bent down to collect the final remnants of the window, a particularly sharp piece nicked her finger, drawing blood.

"Ouch!" she hissed, bringing her injured finger to her lips, tasting the metallic tang. "Perfect start to the day."

Sadie rolled her eyes at the paperwork now scattered throughout the room. "Alright, first things first. Deal with the window," she told herself firmly, picking up the coat rack. Even as the frustration of a now wasted morning lingered, she had no choice but to push it aside and focus on the task at hand. With a heavy sigh, she dressed again and headed out.

Sadie pulled the door of her cabin shut with a huff, her breath turning to frosty clouds. The snow crunched beneath her boots as she trudged through the thick blanket that covered the streets of the small town.

"Morning, Sadie!" called out Mr. Jenkins from across the street, his cheerful voice cutting through the cold like a knife.

"Morning," grumbled Sadie, not bothering to look up from her determined march. She wrapped her arms tighter around herself, her heavy winter coat providing little comfort against the biting wind.

As she approached the town square, the murmur of voices and laughter reached her ears. A knot of townspeople had gathered outside the bakery, steam rising from their mugs of coffee as they chatted animatedly. Among them stood Eleanor Frost, her hawk-like eyes narrowing as soon as they landed on Sadie.

"Ah, there's our dear Sadie Wexford," Eleanor said, loud enough for Sadie to hear despite the din. "Still sulking about, I see."

Sadie gritted her teeth. She could feel the stares of the townspeople on her back as she walked past them, their whispers hanging in the air like icicles.

"Can you believe it?" Eleanor continued, her voice dripping with disdain. "Her poor grandmother must be rolling in her grave, knowing that Sadie's running that candy store into the ground."

"Shame, really," chimed in another woman, sipping from her steaming mug. "The

Snowflake Sugar Shop used to be such a delight."

"Indeed," agreed Eleanor, casting one last disapproving glance at Sadie's retreating form. "I simply don't understand why she insists on clinging to that old place. She should sell it to someone who knows what they're doing."

Sadie's blood boiled beneath her frosty exterior. She hated that Eleanor was right. She didn't know what she was doing. But dammit, she would show them all—the candy store was all she had, and she'd be damned if she allowed anyone, especially Eleanor Frost, to take that away from her. "Let them talk," Sadie muttered under her breath, a fierce determination burning in her chest. "I've survived worse."

With her heart pounding and cheeks flushed from the biting cold, Sadie continued on her way, leaving Eleanor's harsh words behind her. She made her way through the quaint town square, lined with charming wooden storefronts adorned with twinkling fairy lights. "Almost there," she muttered to herself, focusing on the comforting sight of Caleb Winters' general store up ahead.

As Sadie approached the store, the glow from the windows beckoned her inside, like a lighthouse guiding her to safe harbor. She let out a sigh of relief when she finally pushed open the door, stepping into the cozy embrace of the store's interior.

"Morning, Sadie," called out Caleb from behind the counter, his friendly grin lighting up the room. "Bit of a chilly one today, huh?"

"You could say that again," Sadie replied, her scowl softening ever so slightly as she unzipped her parka. The warmth of the store was a welcome contrast to the frosty reception she'd received outside.

Caleb's general store was a haven in the small town, filled with an assortment of goods that catered to every need. Shelves were stocked with everything from fresh produce and canned goods to handmade quilts and knitted mittens. The enticing aroma of freshly brewed coffee mingled with cinnamon and nutmeg created an atmosphere that felt almost magical.

"Let me guess," said Caleb, leaning over the counter with a teasing glint in his eyes. "You're here for my world-famous coffee?"

"Not exactly," Sadie admitted. "But now that I'm here, I'm definitely going to have some."

Caleb poured her a cup of coffee and placed it on the counter. "So, what brings you in today?"

"I need a small piece of plywood and some screws to cover a window I broke this morning. It's only about this big." She held up her hands. "I'm going to need some replacement glass too, but I'll call in the measurements another time."

"Say no more," Caleb grinned. "I've got you covered."

"Thanks, Caleb," Sadie said, turning to survey the store as Caleb went in search of the plywood. The sight of happy customers chatting and laughing with one another filled her with a sense of hope that she seldom allowed herself to feel. If they could find joy in this tiny corner of the world, then perhaps she could, too.

"Sadie," Caleb said, drawing her attention back to him. He leaned a piece of plywood against the counter. "Missy just told me about what Eleanor said to you outside. I hope you're not listening to her. We all know how hard you're working at the candy store."

"Doesn't stop people from talking," Sadie replied, her scowl returning as she thought of Eleanor's cutting words.

"Let them talk," Caleb insisted, his voice firm but gentle. "You've got nothing to prove."

Sadie turned her gaze back toward the window and the snowy streets beyond. "I feel like the entire town is watching my every move, waiting for me to fail."

"Oh, Sadie, no," Caleb said. "And even if people like to gossip, ultimately, the only person's opinion that matters is your own."

Sadie met his steady gaze, feeling a strange mixture of gratitude and frustration welling up inside her. She knew he was right, of course—but accepting that truth was easier said than done.

"Thanks, Caleb, and I hope the advice is free because I might need some more," she joked.

"Anytime," he replied, his eyes warm with understanding. "And advice to friends is always free."

Friends. Huh. Sadie could certainly use one of those.

She paid Caleb and picked up her supplies. Turning to leave the store, she bumped into a young mother, cradling her baby in one arm and carrying a shopping basket with the other.

"Oh," said the woman. "You're Sadie Wexford, aren't you?"

"Yes."

"Well, nice to meet you. I've been meaning to come into the candy store. My mother has been raving about it. Are you open this afternoon?"

"We are. Until six. And I'll pass along your mother's compliments to Rosie."

"Great. We'll be by later." She hoisted the heavy basket onto the counter for Caleb. "See you then."

Sadie nodded, then caught Caleb's eye. "Told you so," he mouthed at her.

Hopefully, he was right.

Chapter 3

W HILE OWNING A CANDY store had never been Sadie's dream career, it was hard not to appreciate the symphony of color and sweetness and how Rosie's carefully crafted confections sang out to passersby—except Eleanor, of course. But, Sadie mused, Caleb might have been right about not everyone waiting for her to fail, as there had been a steady stream of customers recently. So much so that Sadie was busy refilling the candy on a whimsical carousel in the shop's front window.

"Always away from direct sunlight," she said under her breath, mocking Rosie's instructions. "As if that's a problem here."

The door jingled, followed by a gust of icy wind and a man with a jovial countenance, a gap-toothed smile, thick blond hair, and a well-trimmed beard. He shook off the snow that clung to his bright red coat and stomped his feet on the doormat, his breath forming a small cloud in the chilly air as the door closed.

"Good morning!" he boomed, his velvety deep voice filling the store like music. Sadie noted his robust build—he looked like the kind of man who could chop wood for hours without breaking a sweat—and the twinkle in his eye that suggested he held a million secrets.

Too bad she hated secrets.

"Morning," she replied curtly.

"Quite the selection you've got here," the man said, his eyes scanning the colorful display of candies and chocolates. "I must say, I'm impressed."

"Thanks," Sadie said. "We do our best."

"Ah, well, I can see that. My name's Martin Kringle, by the way. I don't believe we've met."

"Kringle? I think you mean Kris Kringle, and I'm not in the mood for jokes."

Martin chuckled, seemingly unfazed by her grumpy demeanor. "Named Martin by my parents. Would you like to see some identification?" He reached into his back pocket for his wallet. "It's my grandfather who's named Kris, and to be honest, it's a traditional family name, but it usually skips a few generations." He held out an Alaskan driver's license.

Sadie squinted at the piece of ID. Sure enough. Martin Kringle.

"My apologies, Mr. Kringle," she replied, her voice clipped and short, reluctant to trust him despite the evidence. Surely that whole Kris Kringle thing was a joke. Having a surname like Kringle at this time of year must get tiresome, and she regretted her previous comments. "So, what can I get for you?"

"Please, call me Martin," he said with a grin. "And I'd like to place a special order. A very large order. In fact, it will take a while to prepare, so I hope there is enough time between now and Christmas Eve."

Sadie raised an eyebrow, her curiosity piqued. Would Eleanor have sent him in as some kind of test? Surely not. The woman was a gossip. Nothing more. "Fine. Let me grab a notepad, and we can go from there."

"Sounds perfect," Martin said, his eyes crinkling due to his enormous smile. "Thank you, Sadie."

"You're welcome. Do you—" Sadie froze. She didn't remember introducing herself. How did he know her name? Oh, she must have told him. Besides, even if she hadn't, the whole town knew who she was. "Do you want to start with some samples?"

"That would be great."

As she began to gather samples and calculate costs, Sadie glanced up at Martin, who was whistling "Santa Claus is Coming to Town" while perusing the shelves. The snow on his red coat had melted, yet it sparkled like ice crystals in the sun. Sadie's stomach churned with butter-flies, giving her an odd sense of anticipation as she again wondered what secrets lay hidden behind his bright eyes and rugged good looks. She shook her head, clearing her mind. *No more sugar for you today.*

"Sadie, you have an enchanting selection here," Martin said, his eyes dancing from display to display. "Tell me, what's the story behind these striped candies?"

"Peppermint twists," Sadie replied. If this man did have secrets, she didn't want to know about them. All secrets did was cause pain. "And there's no story. Rosie makes them using my grandmother's recipe. They're a popular choice during the holidays."

"Ah, wonderful! I can imagine how delightful they would taste after a long day in the cold," Martin exclaimed, his enthusiasm almost infectious. Almost.

"Suppose so," Sadie mumbled, uncomfortable with the way she enjoyed the rich tone of his voice.

As he moved through the store, Martin continued to inquire about the various candies and chocolates. Sadie met each question with a brief and direct response. Yet, Martin remained undeterred by her reluctance to engage in conversation.

"Ooh, what are these little ones here?" he asked, pointing at a display of tiny, brightly colored candies.

"Jelly buttons," Sadie answered, her tone slightly less frosty than before, humored by his child-like enthusiasm. "They're fruit-flavored, quite popular with children." Sadie picked up one with some tongs and dropped it into Martin's hand.

"Delightful!" Martin beamed, popping it into his mouth. "Mmm, that's delicious! You truly have a gift, Sadie."

"Thanks, but as I said before, Rosie does all the candy making."

"Well then, please pass on my compliments to your confectioner. Now, tell me about these chocolates," Martin continued, gesturing towards a tray of elaborately decorated confections. "They look positively divine."

"Handcrafted truffles," Sadie explained, her interest growing, not only by his genuine fascination, but by his diction. He didn't sound like a local. "Each one is filled with a different flavored ganache. It takes time to make them, but they're worth it."

"The attention to detail is extraordinary," Martin said. "I can see why the Snowflake Sugar Shop has such a devoted following."

"What do you mean?" Sadie questioned. "Our customers are mostly locals and the occasional tourist," Sadie admitted. "But apparently, my grandmother was very proud of what she'd built."

"As you should be," Martin agreed, his sincere smile never leaving his face. "It's not often you come across such a treasure trove of sweet delights." Martin pulled out his phone and showed Sadie the social media pages. "You've never seen this?"

"Well, no. I mean, I knew Rosie was posting, but I steer clear of social media."

Martin nodded as if he understood, then scrolled through the Snowflake Sugar Shop's images.

"They're amazing," Sadie whispered. For the first time in what felt like ages, she smiled. Not only was Rosie a talented confectioner, her ability to photograph the candy was equally impressive, and their following was incredible.

"This caught our attention," Martin said. "A small town with this kind of candy store was the place we wanted to set up shop."

"You're new here too?" Sadie asked.

"We are. I'm a toymaker. We're the ones renovating the store across the town square. Our old one was outside of a town north of here, but it burned down in the forest fires last summer."

"I'm so sorry to hear that."

"No one was hurt, and we've moved many times before, so we're used to it," he replied with a hearty chuckle, his gap-toothed grin widening even further. "Now, let's get down to business, shall we?"

Sadie and Martin sat at a small table near the back of the store, surrounded by the scent of sweet confections. Despite her usual reticence, she couldn't help but be drawn to him, as this ruggedly handsome, unusually spoken toymaker was also an outsider in this close-knit town.

"Alright, Martin," Sadie began, tugging at the hem of her apron, "tell me more about this large order."

Martin rubbed the back of his neck. "Well, you see, I have an important event coming up, and I'd love to include your delightful confections as part of it."

"An event?" Sadie asked, tilting her head. Her skepticism resurfacing at the vagueness of his reply.

"Indeed. You could say it's a celebration of sorts."

"This time of year is full of events." She tapped her pen impatiently on the table. "All I need are the details. When and how much?"

He leaned back in his chair, studying her intently. "Well, I come from a long line of toymakers, and my family has always been involved in special events during the holiday season."

"Ah," Sadie said, raising an eyebrow suspiciously. "And this event...is it for charity or something?" If it was, he'd likely ask for a reduced rate, and Sadie wasn't sure they could afford that. They were barely scraping by as it was.

"Something like that," Martin answered, his grin widening. "It's a tradition, you see, spreading joy and cheer to children who might not have much else to look forward to."

Sadie eyed him warily, trying to piece together the puzzle that was Martin Kringle. He was undeniably warm and charismatic, yet there was a mysterious air about him that kept her on edge. "And let me guess, your workshop is full of Santa's elves."

He tilted his head back and let out a hearty laugh. "Grandfather said you were funny."

"Grandfather? Who's your grandfather?"

"He was in the other day. Big white beard."

"Right. I remember him. He was buying candy for his grandkids. Wait. Aren't you a bit old for that?"

"It was for business only. We all had to taste the candy before we placed an order this large. And your confections passed with flying colors."

"So, all of you run one little toy store?"

"Not quite. We're more of an international conglomerate. The history of toy making goes back generations. We started with a single workshop but soon found it was too hard to keep up with production. Smaller factories in strategic locations worked far better. There are eight locations and each one is run by one of the grandchildren. I," he smiled, leaning back in the chair, "work in North America-West."

"Right then," she said, relieved that there must be some money backing his purchase. "What kind of numbers are we talking about?"

Martin reached into his breast pocket and pulled out a piece of paper. He handed it to Sadie. She blinked in disbelief, then glared at

Martin. "I knew it. This is a joke. Did Eleanor send you?"

"No joke," he said, his expression serious as he handed her a check. "This should cover about half the cost. We'll pay the rest upon delivery."

Sadie stared at the check. Holy crap. This order would save the store.

And then some.

Chapter 4

MARTIN SAT FACING HIS grandfather across a large mahogany desk, his laptop open. "So, how did it go?" his grandfather asked, peering up at him through his thick-rimmed glasses. The old man's office was cramped, especially with that beast of a desk, but each visit filled Martin with a sense of nostalgia—the smell of leather-bound books, the sound of the clock ticking in the corner, and the sight of his grandfather's old typewriter, still perched atop a wooden pedestal took Martin back to his childhood. He'd spent many an afternoon in that room while his father and grandfather discussed business.

"It went well," Martin replied. "Sadie agreed to supply us with candy."

"Good," his grandfather said, nodding. "I remember when her grandmother ran the shop. You could always rely on her for good candy."

"You've done business with the Snowflake Sugar Shop before? I thought they were new suppliers."

"Oh, they are, but Mable, Sadie's grandmother, gave us a hand from time to time. Until recently, I didn't know that Mable had a granddaughter, but the family resemblance is strong. Sadie's the spitting image of her grandmother."

Martin smiled. "Is she? I hope Mable was friendlier."

His grandfather chuckled. "She was. And yes, Sadie is a bit grumpy, but maybe all she needs is a little Christmas magic." He glanced at Martin over the top of his glasses.

Martin nodded. "I like her, though. Her skepticism kept me on my toes."

He couldn't help but think about Sadie's piercing blue eyes and how they looked right through him. Something about her certainly interested him, although he couldn't put his finger on anything specific. Maybe it was the way she carried herself, with an air of confidence—no, make that indifference—that was both intriguing and intimidating. "I think there's more to her than meets the eye."

"What do you mean?" his grandfather asked, leaning forward.

"Oh, I don't know exactly. It's just a feeling I have."

Martin's grandfather nodded thoughtfully. "Could be. But it's not our place to pry. All we need is a strong business relationship. Now, let's take a look at the numbers." His grandfather gestured to the laptop screen. Together, they pored over the budget for the season, factoring in the cost of Sadie's candy. Martin was grateful for his grandfather's guidance. He couldn't imagine running things without him.

As they worked, Martin's mind kept drifting back to Sadie. He wondered what her life was like outside the candy shop. Did she have family nearby? A partner? Did she enjoy the store, or was it merely a job?

"Martin? Are you listening?" his grandfather's voice broke through his thoughts.

"Sorry, what was that?"

"I said that we need to monitor the bottom line. We can't go overboard on the candy order."

"Right, of course," Martin said, refocusing on the screen. "I'll make sure everything is within budget."

As they finished up their work, Martin's thoughts returned to Sadie. He wondered if he would see her again soon. Maybe he could bring her a cup of coffee or something to show his appreciation for her help. Assumably, the order was larger than the store was accustomed to handling. Yet, he'd seen nothing but determination in her eyes—after the skepticism, that is.

Martin closed his laptop and stood. "Thanks, Grandpa. I'll make sure to keep you updated on the village's progress. We've chosen a great location a few miles out of town. Now that construction has begun, the holofield is in place. The site is completely hidden."

"And the toy store in town?"

"Slow but steady. The village is taking most of our efforts."

"As it should. Great job, Martin. I'm proud of you." His grandfather smiled, his eyes filled with pride. "Now, don't let me keep you any longer. I know you're busy."

As Martin packed up his laptop and headed out of his grandfather's office, his thoughts turned again to Sadie. He was determined to find out what was behind her standoffish demeanor.

Several hours after Martin Kringle's visit, Sadie stood behind the counter of her candy store, wrapping a fresh batch of peppermint sticks in shiny cellophane. The frosty air outside had left a delicate layer of condensation on the windows, blurring the view of the snow-covered town beyond into a watercolor painting.

"Who knew a candy order could be so...int eresting?" she mused, because she'd enjoyed her morning festively wrapping candy. Did Martin expect this level of detail? If so, they'd have to hire a few more people. As it was, Sadie had no idea if Rosie could handle the large order. The thought of that upcoming conversation made her nervous.

She'd wrapped a few more peppermint sticks when the door opened and Sadie looked up, surprised to see Rosie.

"Good morning, Sadie," Rosie said with her usual smile. "Looks like you've been busy."

"I have, and I'm glad you came in early. We have a lot to discuss."

Rosie's complexion turned gray. "You're closing the store."

"What? No." Sadie shook her head, confused. "Why would you think that?"

Rosie shrugged, avoiding eye contact. "I don't know. Rumors, I guess."

"Eleanor," Sadie hissed. "Well, that's not the case. Quite the opposite, actually. We have a big candy order to fill from a Mr. Kringle."

Rosie's face brightened at the mention of the order. "The man building the toy store?"

"That's the one."

"Holy candy corn, that's fabulous."

Sadie gave her a closed-lip smile. "You haven't seen how big yet." She handed the order to Rosie, and Sadie thought Rosie's big green eyes were going to pop right out of her head.

"You're kidding, right?"

"No. I'm not."

Rosie collapsed on a stool behind the cash desk. "This is a lot of candy, and when I say a lot, I mean like a mountain's worth. Come on, Sadie. I'm good, but I'm not that good."

"There's still a couple of weeks, and I'll help, and we'll hire some extra hands if we need to. The store needs this, Rosie. And if we succeed, it might be the piece of Christmas magic that makes me believe, and you'd win our bet."

Rosie covered her face with her hands and exhaled loudly. Then she peeked at Sadie between the gaps in her fingers. "We're going to need a lot of Christmas magic to get this done."

"Yay." Sadie clapped her hands. "Thank you."

Rosie raised an eyebrow.

"What?"

"You're smiling. Have I won already?"

Sadie's cheeks turned red. "No. And it's not impossible for me to smile, you know. I've smiled once or twice in the past." But that was before her life in Florida blew up, and she certainly didn't want to tell Rosie about that.

The next morning, Sadie arranged the candy displays with a newfound determination. Martin's candy order was a lifeline. Not only that, although she hated to admit it, she also couldn't shake the memory of Martin's kind and sincere smile. It was a stark contrast to her final few weeks in Florida, where people she encountered either snickered or turned away altogether.

"Good morning, Miss Wexford," came a cheerful voice from behind her, causing Sadie to jump slightly. She turned to see Mrs. Anderson, one of her regular customers, eyeing the candies with delight. "These new arrangements are absolutely enchanting."

"You know Rosie. She's a rare talent."

"You are so right, my dear," said Mrs. Anderson. "Well, I'm going to pick up eight of these chocolate truffles. I have the ladies over for bridge today, and these are absolutely mouthwatering."

"Great," Sadie said and packed them up. Mrs. Anderson knew everyone, but she wasn't a gossip like Eleanor. Should she ask about Martin Kringle? "I...had an interesting visitor yesterday. A toymaker named Martin Kringle."

"Ah, yes!" Mrs. Anderson exclaimed, her eyes lighting up with recognition. "I've heard of him. A very kind man, they say, but quite mysterious."

Sadie leaned in closer. "Mysterious? How so?"

"Well, I've never met him myself, but the rumors say he's a bit...magical, if you can believe it," Mrs. Anderson whispered conspiratorially.

"Magical?" Sadie scoffed, her skepticism flaring up. "There's no such thing."

"Perhaps not," Mrs. Anderson replied, her smile unwavering. "But one can't help but wonder, can they? And we can use a little magic around here. We lost three businesses from Main Street this year. Thank goodness you took over your grandmother's store, and thank goodness for Mr. Kringle. Without more new investment, this town will disappear from the map."

"Oh, that's awful." And no pressure. Did Mrs. Anderson seriously place the burden of saving the town on Sadie's shoulders? And Martin's?

Sadie smiled tightly as Mrs. Anderson paid for her confections and left the store. Stress tightened her chest. Sadie had inherited the store. If it failed, she was hardly to blame. The store was barely breaking even when she'd taken over, and what could she, someone completely new to the business—let alone the town—do to improve things? And what about Martin Kringle? Did he realize the hopes that were pinned to his success? If he did, would he still be so jolly? *Jolly?* Since when did she start using words like jolly?

All this Christmas talk must be wearing off on her.

"It won't take magic to save this town," she said to the empty store. "It will take a miracle."

Chapter 5

"HERE YOU GO, SWEETIE," Martin said, placing a plate of pancakes in front of his daughter, Nora. "Eat up."

"Thanks, Dad. Pancakes are my favorite." She took a big bite. "Are you going to the candy store today to check on your order?"

"I might." Martin sat across from her, taking a sip of his coffee.

"Can I come?"

"Sure. If you'd like to."

Nora eyed him suspiciously. "That was too easy."

"What do you mean?"

"Well, typically, there's more resistance when I suggest taking me out into the big, bad world."

"I do not call it that."

Nora rolled her eyes. "Dad, relax. I'm joking. But seriously, normally I ask, and you say, 'I don't know. We have to be careful,' and then I say, 'I'm fourteen and know not to let the cat out of the bag,' and you say, 'let me think about it,' before you agree and the lecture about me eventually taking over the business begins."

"I don't do that." Martin thought for a moment. "Okay, maybe I do, but we can't take our responsibility too lightly."

"Yeah, I know. But since you were so quick to agree this time, does that mean they know who you are?"

"No, sweetie, they don't."

"Are you going to tell them? They're working for you."

Martin scratched his beard. "You know it's not that simple."

"Mom knew."

"Well, of course mom knew. We'd known each other since we were kids. You know that. My relationship with the candy store is strictly business. And even if it wasn't, it's difficult for people to accept that our family is...different."

"Dad, you're Santa. Everyone loves Santa."

Martin chuckled. "True, but I'm not *the* Santa. I'm *a* Santa, along with my siblings and cousins, right? So, even on the slightest chance that someone believes me, they'd find it hard to accept the reality over what they know from lore."

"I guess," Nora said, taking a bite of pancake. "But what's baffling is that the legend assumes that only one person delivers all the gifts all over the world in one night."

"Agreed," Martin said and ruffled his daughter's hair.

"Dad, I'm not a kid. You're going to mess up my hair."

"Sorry, sweetie." Sometimes raising a teenager was more exhausting than Christmas Eve.

Nora finished her breakfast and helped Martin clean up the dishes before they bundled up in their coats and scarves and set off toward the candy store. Thoughts of the next couple of weeks preoccupied Martin on their journey into town. Since his village and toy factory were under construction, they had to import their toys from the other Santa villages. Luckily, his assistant, Ellie, had a business degree specializing in logistics. He'd check in with her later.

But first, he had to make sure the candy order was in top shape.

As they approached the store, they could see Sadie and Rosie through the window, surrounded by stacks of candy boxes and wrapping paper. Nora's eyes widened as she took in the scene. "Wow, Dad, they really are making a lot of candy."

Martin chuckled. "Yes, they are. Let's go say hi."

"This place is amazing," Nora said as they walked in.

Martin smiled and headed to the counter, where Sadie and Rosie were busy packing boxes of peppermint candy. "Good morning," he said.

Sadie glanced up and smiled. Martin realized she'd been so focused, he'd caught her off guard, and for a brief instant, her smile had been soft, radiating warmth like a candle flame. Sadly, it disappeared as quickly as it appeared.

"Good morning, Martin. How can I help you today?"

Martin stood there, still as a statue, frozen in his musings. His eyes were distant and unfocused, drawn to the slight curve of her lips as she spoke. He wondered if he could make it happen again—that moment when her mouth curved up into a genuine smile.

"Dad," Nora whispered, giving him a gentle elbow to the gut.

"Oh, right. Good morning, ladies. My daughter Nora, here, was curious about the candy order, so I told her I'd bring her in."

"Well, nice to meet you, Nora. I'm Sadie, and this is Rosie. Rosie is the one you can thank for all this delicious candy." Sadie turned to face Martin. "It's coming along nicely. There is still a ton to make, but we're getting there."

"I have no doubt it will all get done," Martin said. "And Rosie, it's a pleasure to meet you in person. I'm a huge fan of your Instagram page."

"Thank you," Rosie said, her cheeks reddening. "And you're the man whose candy order practically gave me a heart attack."

Martin held up his hands in surrender. "Guilty as charged."

Rosie laughed, then turned to Nora. "Nora, would you give us a hand?"

Nora's eyes lit up. "Really? I can help?"

"That's a great idea," Sadie said. "We could use all the help we can get. How about you help us wrap some of these boxes?"

Nora nodded eagerly and joined Sadie and Rosie at the wrapping station. For a moment, Martin forgot about the stresses of the season, the work that lay ahead, and the secret he kept hidden from almost everyone in the world. He simply enjoyed watching his daughter wrap candy.

"If you're going to stand there, you may as well help."

"What?" he asked, Sadie's voice snapping him out of the moment.

"I said if you're just going to stand there, wash your hands, grab an apron, and get to work." Her tone was stiff, but he could make out the tiniest hint of humor.

"All right then," Martin said, Sadie's quip making him feel like one of the community. A regular person. He rolled up his sleeves. "I'll show you what this old toymaker can do."

There it was again. Sadie's brief but genuine smile pierced his heart like the first beam of sunlight after a long, dark night. As they worked, Martin couldn't help but notice how Sadie's eyes sparkled one moment, then turned distant and unreadable the next. It was as if she forgot her worries for a moment, then remembered and her armor would go up like a force field. He had secrets, but they weren't painful, merely inconvenient. Sadie, on the other hand, had been hurt.

After an hour of hard work, Martin's phone buzzed. He read the text. "Nora, we're needed at the toy store. Time to go."

"But Dad, can't the...crew figure it out on their own?"

"Afraid not. Great-Grandpa's meeting us there."

"But Dad," Nora continued.

Martin placed a hand on her shoulder. "Nora, you know you need to learn the business if you are to take over one day."

"I know. And I told you the lecture would begin at some point," she said. "But what if I don't want to follow in the family business? What if I want to make candy instead?"

"Then you will make candy, but for now, you need to come. Anything you learn can apply to whatever you choose to do. Remember that."

"Okay," Nora said, her voice full of resignation. "Thank you," she said to Sadie and Rosie. "I had a great time. Maybe I can help again?"

"Absolutely. We're going to need all the help we can get," Rosie said.

"Yes," Sadie said in agreement. "You're both welcome back anytime."

Martin gave them a quick nod. "Thank you, ladies." He then ushered Nora outside before turning to give one last wave.

He just might take Sadie up on that offer.

Chapter 6

S ADIE'S FINGERS DEFTLY TWISTED the gold paper around another chocolate truffle, her movements fluid and precise. The Snowflake Sugar Shop was alive with the scents of sugar and cinnamon, making her wonder what Grandma Mable would think. She wished they could have met, but it wasn't from lack of trying on her grandmother's part. When Grandma Mable gave her father up for adoption, she'd been young and naïve and agreed to a sealed adoption. At least according to the attorney Sadie had spoken to. By the time her grandmother had discovered her father's last known whereabouts, he'd been dead for several years. And Grandma Mable was ill herself. With little time left, she'd changed her will and given the store to her only grandchild, Sadie.

There was no one to be mad at. No letters or diaries left behind, and no one to ask since Grandma Mabel had moved to Mistletoe in her senior year of high school, one year after Sadie's father had been born. The people of Mistletoe were almost as surprised at the revelation as Sadie herself, Rosie had told her.

And while she initially viewed the inheritance simply as her ticket out of Miami, Sadie now wanted to make this unknown grandmother proud. She'd learn to run the store, but fitting in proved more challenging. There was her disdain for the cold and outdoor activities in general. She'd avoided Bingo night, the town square clean-up event, and the Thanksgiving parade. She'd also declined the invitation to join the Main Street Business Improvement Committee. All that was on her, but she'd had the sinking feeling that people were keeping their distance. An all too painful reminder of the way her friends ghosted her as her life fell apart in Miami. That pain cut deep. Very deep. And she didn't want to relive anything like it again. So keeping her distance kept her safe.

The bell above the door jingled merrily, announcing a customer. Sadie's gaze flicked up, and she recognized the unmistakable lumberjack form of Martin Kringle immediately. Clutched in his hand were two steaming lattes, the aroma of fresh espresso mingling with the sugary air.

"Good evening, Sadie," Martin greeted, his voice as jovial as ever. "I thought you might enjoy a little pick-me-up on this chilly day."

"Thank you," Sadie responded.

"Of course. It's the least I could do after your kindness yesterday," Martin replied, his eyes twinkling as if sharing a private joke with her.

Sadie allowed herself a small nod—an unspoken acceptance of his offering. After all, it would be rude to turn down such a gesture of gratitude. As her fingers wrapped around the warm cup, she inhaled the enticing aroma of caramel and cinnamon. She took a tentative sip and found herself pleasantly surprised by the drink's sweetness—it seemed Martin had an uncanny knack for knowing her preferences.

"While I appreciate the gesture, I simply helped a customer," she said.

"Ah, but you and Rosie went above and beyond," Martin insisted, leaning against the counter. "Not many would have taken the time to let a young girl and a frazzled single father help wrap candies."

"Really, it was nothing," Sadie muttered, turning away from his charismatic smile. She wrapped her hands around the latte, enjoying the heat on her icy fingers. "And you both helped us, so let's say it was win-win."

"Win-win. I like that," Martin replied, taking a sip of his latte.

The room filled with silence. "Is there something you need?" she asked cautiously.

"Nothing more than to express my gratitude," Martin replied and turned to leave.

The sincerity in his tone disarmed her slightly. "Wait for me," Sadie said impulsively. "I'm done for the day and was going to leave soon. Hang on, and I'll walk you out. That is if you don't mind waiting while I lock up." *Walk you out?* What was she thinking? It was about three yards to the door.

Martin's smile could have melted all the snow in Alaska. "I don't mind. Can I help?"

"No. I'll just be a minute. Rosie cleaned and did the prep for tomorrow. I was simply puttering around," Sadie said over the rustle of candy wrappers as she closed the box and put the tray of truffles in the cooler.

Sadie finished quickly and found Martin leaning on the counter once more. She stood on the other side, studying the steam escaping from the small hole in the latte lid, feeling its warmth against her cheeks. Martin's expression exuded patience, as if he expected her to speak.

"Being a single father must be tough," she said, breaking the silence as she traced the rim of the cup with her thumb. "Especially when you're also running a business."

"Indeed," Martin replied. "Between juggling work and taking care of my daughter, it can be quite overwhelming." He paused, glancing out the window at the flurry of snowflakes swirling outside. "But, somehow, we manage."

She could feel the heaviness of his words, the weight that responsibility laid upon his broad shoulders. "Sounds like you've got your hands full."

"I do, yes, but I have a large family and am close to my employees at the toy store, so there are always people around to help. You know what they say, it takes a village and all that." Martin chuckled, but Sadie noted a touch of sadness behind his laughter. "We lost my wife when Nora was only two." He shook his head, the corners of his mouth twitching downward. "Since then, it's been difficult trying to balance it all."

"I'm so sorry," Sadie said, taking a sip of coffee. Memories of her own childhood now stirred within. Before she could stop herself, she said, "I remember my dad working long hours, struggling to keep our family afloat after Mom left."

Martin's eyes melted into pools of compassion. "I'm truly sorry, Sadie," he whispered, reaching out, placing his rugged hand on her arm, and giving her a reassuring squeeze.

Whether it was her earlier rumination about her grandmother or the way his charming smile broke through her defenses, she couldn't be sure. All she knew was that a cascade of raw emotion burst forth, like a river unleashed from its bounds. "That's why I can't buy into this whole facade of Christmas joy. It feels so hollow. As if your troubles disappear simply because it's Christmas. My mom left us shortly after Christmas when I was ten. But we spent the holidays as if everything was fine. She pretended the entire time. Smiling. Laughing. We made plans for the rest of the holidays. But she was gone before New Year's Eve. And it felt like our family had been nothing but an illusion."

Tears streamed down her face as she drew a shaky breath. More than anything, she wanted to stop talking, yet the pain and betrayal within her clamored for freedom, demanding to be heard. And there, amidst the storm of her emotions, stood Martin, a beacon of patience, his presence obliterating any hope she had of stopping.

"A few years ago, my father passed away from cancer. They discovered it way too late, and he had little time. Instead of telling me immediately, he waited until after Christmas, not wanting to spoil the holidays. But the deception made it worse. I would have spent more time with him instead of spending it with my friends." Friends who had let her down when she needed them most.

With that memory, the hurt dissolved, and anger took its place, flooding her thoughts with images of last Christmas. "And then there was..." She stopped. Unable to say his name, but more than capable of remembering the shock of finding him with another woman. Worse than that discovery, was that she didn't face it alone. The reality show camera crew had been on her heels and had captured everything.

Overwhelmed with embarrassment, she suddenly realized she stood in the middle of the store. "I'm so sorry," she murmured, distressed. "Talking about the single dad situation must have triggered this. I don't usually unravel like this." She spoke the truth. It was uncommon, but the last time had been very, very public. "You probably wish you'd never brought me that coffee now, huh?"

"Not at all," Martin said, then took a step toward Sadie and wrapped her in a hug.

At first she stiffened, still embarrassed about her breakdown, but then as the seconds passed, she found comfort in his embrace. The heat of his body, the beating of his heart, the way his beard scratched the top of her head, the way he held her, simply to comfort. She read no judgment in any of his actions, and that nearly made her cry anew.

"Sometimes talking to a stranger is easier than those closest to us," Martin said.

Sadie nodded against his chest. "I have a lot of baggage."

"Well, is it any lighter now? You emptied some of those bags all over the floor."

Giving him a small laugh, Sadie reluctantly withdrew from his embrace. "A bit, maybe. Yes. Thanks."

"I have an idea," he said. "Something that might make you feel better."

"I don't know," she said as her walls that had crumbled began to rebuild.

"Trust me," he said, passing Sadie her coat, then extending his hand.

She hesitated, but at that moment, as they stood amidst the sweet scents of the candy store, their connection felt both tangible and powerful—so Sadie pulled on her parka, reached out, and took his hand.

Chapter 7

S ADIE ENTERED THE BRISK night air, her fingers interlaced tightly with Martin's. As they rounded the corner beside her quaint little shop, the enchanting sight that lay ahead rendered her speechless. There, nestled between the shadows and bathed in the silvery glow of the moon, was a magnificent sleigh, its intricate carvings and polished woodwork reflecting the celestial light. It was the kind of sleigh she had read about in fiction and imagined in dreams.

Before it stood a majestic reindeer, its coat glossy and deep brown, muscles flexing with every subtle movement. The reindeer's impressive antlers, which seemed to stretch towards the starry heavens, were dusted with frost, making them sparkle. With every gentle exhale, it released puffs of breath that crystallized immediately, creating tiny, fleeting clouds.

Sadie, voice quivering, asked, "Is this a dream?"

"As real as the dreams that keep joy alive. Climb aboard," Martin said, his eyes reflecting the depth of the starry night.

"No, seriously. What kind of toymaker travels in a reindeer-drawn sleigh?"

"An environmentally friendly one. And it's an elk. Not a reindeer."

"Right. Of course," Sadie replied. Her tone dripped with sarcasm. "So, this is how you get around?"

"Mostly. When there's snow. Yes." He gave the elk a pat, then climbed aboard. "Are you coming?"

"I don't know about this." She looked around. What if he were a sociopath? Were there any witnesses to see her leave with him?

"I'm not dangerous," he said as if he could read her mind. "I'm just old school."

"Please don't make me regret this," Sadie said, placing her hand in Martin's. As they began down the street, Sadie found the world fading away. The brisk wind danced around them, but the carriage remained warm, as if enveloping them in a protective cocoon. As they left town behind, the canopy of trees twinkled as if lit by Christmas lights, and right when Sadie thought the scenery couldn't get any prettier, the sky opened up to reveal the awe-inspiring spectacle of the Northern Lights.

Sadie gasped.

Martin led them to a clearing atop a small hill and drew the sleigh to a stop, providing them an unhindered view of the ephemeral beauty of the aurora. For the longest time, they sat in silence while nature's ethereal ballet danced across the vast expanse of the night sky in a mesmerizing display of color and light.

"They're like brushstrokes," Sadie whispered. "Or like a tapestry of greens and purples." It was as if the heavens themselves were reaching out, intertwining with the Earth in a passionate embrace.

To Sadie, the world receded to this single moment under the aurora's spell. Nothing existed outside its splendor. She slid her hand into Martin's, and her eyes teared up. "I've never seen anything like this before."

Martin leaned his head closer, his breath caressing Sadie's ear as he whispered, "Watching the auroras is like listening to a silent love song sung by the stars, a serenade that evokes a sense of wonder, magic, and an intimate connection to the universe."

Sadie shivered, nodding in agreement with this lumberjack poet.

And as silence again blanketed them, she knew it was the kind that spoke more than words ever could because they were both lost in the moment. Sadie suspected that Martin's heart, too, was beating in rhythm with the flickering lights.

Martin's phone buzzed, shattering the moment like a dropped snow globe. "Sorry," he said. "I told them to text me only in an emergency." He glanced at his phone. "Nora's not well. She has a fever. I doubt it's serious, but I better get home."

"Of course," Sadie said, even though she longed to remain there with him. "I understand."

Martin flicked the reins, and the elk moved forward. As the sleigh glided toward Sadie's house, she leaned in, resting her head on Martin's shoulder, finding comfort in the moment's beauty and the gentle strength of her mysterious companion.

As they pulled up in front of her house, Martin climbed out of the sleigh first, holding out his hand for Sadie. He helped her down and escorted her to her front door.

"Thank you, Martin," she said. "Your kindness is a rare gift, and I'm grateful to have met you."

"The pleasure was mine," he said, staring deep into her eyes before placing a chaste kiss on her cheek and wishing her a good night.

His simple gesture of friendship touched her deeply. Under the mesmerizing dance of the Northern Lights, it would have been all too easy to surrender to the whispers of romance. But Sadie, still tender from the scars of recent experience, knew it would take time before she could bravely open the gates of her heart again.

As she unlocked the door, she turned to wave, but Martin and his sleigh were nowhere to be seen.

Martin walked into his daughter's room, placing a cool glass of water beside her bed. "How are you feeling this morning?"

"Not great, but better." Nora sat up and took a drink of water.

"Well, take it easy for the rest of the day. I'm going into work, but Ellie's here to check on you."

"I'm sorry I ruined your date last night, Dad."

Martin sat on the edge of Nora's bed. "It wasn't a date."

"Oh really? Then what was it?"

"Two friends observing the Northern Lights." He thought of Sadie's head on his shoulder, her hand in his, and the pain he wanted to heal.

"Yeah, in an elk-drawn sleigh. I'm sure Sadie does that kind of thing with all her friends."

"Come on, Nora, you know that I have to take things slowly with all that's at stake."

Nora sighed. "Yeah, yeah, I know."

"But just so you know, I like her and would like to get to know her better." His expression turned serious. "Does it bother you that I hope things move forward with Sadie?"

Nora yawned and laid back down. Martin brought her covers up and tucked her in.

"Read the room, Dad. No. Mom's been gone a long time. Don't you think it's time to move on?

I know you won't forget her, but you have to live your life."

He leaned down and kissed Nora on her warm forehead. "How did you get to be so wise?"

"My future self has children's happiness riding on her shoulders. That makes you grow up fast." Nora rolled onto her side. "And since I can't go to the light festival tonight, take Sadie."

"I wasn't planning on attending the festival. There's so much to do."

"The crew is on schedule. Ellie told me so. Now go. For me." She batted her eyelashes.

Martin released an exaggerated sigh. "You know I can never say no to you."

As he departed from Nora's room, an odd sensation struck him, a premonition almost, that one day, he would also find it near impossible to say no to Sadie.

Chapter 8

T HE BELL ABOVE THE door jingled merrily as Martin entered the Snowflake Sugar Shop, shaking off a dusting of snowflakes from his scarf. The aroma of chocolate and peppermint swirled in the air, enveloping Sadie as she stood behind the counter, arranging candy canes with meticulous precision.

"Good afternoon, Sadie," Martin called out, his gap-toothed smile as warm as the lights strung across the store's windowsill.

"Hi, Martin." Sadie couldn't stop the smile that began blossoming on her cheeks. Not with the memory of their sleigh ride under the Northern

Lights so fresh in her mind. "What brings you here today?"

"Well," he began, glancing at the floor before looking at Sadie, "I was wondering if you'd like to accompany me to the opening of the light festival tonight? Nora is still under the weather but insisted I attend, and I'd hate to go alone."

Sadie hesitated momentarily, her fingers tightening around the candy cane in her hand. She empathized with his reluctance to go solo; she also unliked attending events by herself. Perhaps they, both newcomers in this quaint town, could support one another.

"Sounds nice," she replied, setting the candy canes down. "I'd love to go to the light festival with you."

"Really?" Martin's eyes lit up, reflecting the colorful array of sweets that adorned the shelves of the candy store. "Thank you, Sadie. I promise it will be worth your time."

"It better be," she teased.

"Oh, I promise," he said. "Let's say I meet you here at six?"

"It's a date."

"Ready?" Martin asked, holding the door open for her.

"Ready as I'll ever be," Sadie said, trying to ignore the flutter of excitement that stirred within her chest. She couldn't explain it, but there was something about Martin that made her feel as if she were stepping into a world she'd long forgotten. "I can't believe I'm voluntarily spending more time in the cold and snow."

"Sadie," Martin said, his hand on the small of her back. "Once you experience some Christmas magic, you'll forget all about the cold."

"Is that a promise?" she asked playfully, zipping up her jacket as they stepped out into winter's frosty embrace.

"It is," Martin said, his eyes sparkling with what Sadie believed to be mischief.

Once outside, a hastily walking figure nearly bumped right into them.

"Watch where you're going," a sharp voice called out as the figure drew to a stop. Sadie sighed. She knew exactly who that voice belonged to.

Eleanor Frost stood on the sidewalk, her eyes scanning the block before settling on Sadie and Martin. Despite the chill outside, she seemed unaffected by the cold, her graying hair pulled back into a tight bun.

"Oh, Sadie. I'm surprised you're heading to the light festival tonight."

"And why is that, Eleanor?"

"Well, you're a big city girl, aren't you? Surely, our little town's display will be nothing short of disappointing."

"I thought the Mistletoe Light Festival and Christmas Market brought in tourists from all over."

"Well, yes. At least it used to. But each year the crowds grow smaller. And now, it appears our city council has run out of funds for this year's festivities. They're saying not to expect much from the light festival tonight."

"Yes, I heard that rumor," Martin said. "But sometimes it's not about the grandeur of the event. It's the company we share it with." He flashed Sadie a smile.

"Indeed," Eleanor sniffed, giving both Martin and Sadie a pointed look. "Anyway, I thought you should know."

"Thank you, Eleanor," Sadie replied tersely, forcing a smile. "We'll keep that in mind."

With a nod, Eleanor continued on her way, leaving Sadie and Martin alone once more. Sadie sighed, crossing her arms. "Why do I have the feeling she only came here to ruin my mood?"

"Because that's her way," Martin chuckled. "But don't let her words bother you. Tonight will still be marvelous, with or without an extravagant display."

"Let's hope so," Sadie said, but with Martin by her side, she thought that might be true.

The square was full. Sadie hadn't seen that many people in one spot since she'd left Miami. Small vendor booths lined the outside of the square, and the air hummed with excited chatter as families bundled in winter coats gathered around, eagerly anticipating the start of the light festival. The night buzzed with energy, and despite the cold, excitement fluttered in her stomach.

"Attention, everyone!" Mayor Gregory Evergreen announced from a small podium, his confident voice cutting through the chatter. "I have a surprise for you all. Earlier today, we received an anonymous donation of lights for our festival, and our team has been working tirelessly to string them up for your enjoyment."

The crowd murmured in anticipation, and Sadie wondered who the mysterious donor could be. She glanced at Martin.

"Without further ado," the mayor continued, "let us begin our annual light festival."

As the townsfolk erupted into cheers, Sadie felt Martin's hand gently brush against hers. She hesitated for a moment before allowing her fingers to intertwine with his, their affection mingling in the frigid air.

"Ready?" Martin asked, squeezing her hand, his smile growing larger.

"Ready," Sadie replied. Inspired by his enthusiasm and excitement, Sadie let go of the hurt and skepticism triggered by the holiday season. It was time to simply enjoy.

"Let the countdown begin," the mayor ordered.

"Three, two, one!" the crowd shouted, and the mayor flipped the switch.

The town square erupted into a breathtaking spectacle of shimmering lights, casting an ethereal glow over the snow-covered ground. Gasps of wonderment rose from the crowd as they gazed up at the enchanting display that danced across the night sky.

"It's...it's beautiful," Sadie whispered, her eyes wide with awe as she took in the scene before her. "I wasn't expecting such a striking display, were you?"

"No. This is even better than I imagined," Martin replied.

As they gazed at the mesmerizing lights, a thought flickered through Sadie's mind. Could it be? Was it possible that Martin was the anonymous donor? But why would he keep it a secret?

"Who do you think did this?" she ventured.

"That doesn't matter, does it? What's important is that they made our little town magical tonight," Martin answered.

Sadie studied his face, searching for any signs that might betray his involvement in the donation. He'd avoided a direct response, but his expression remained unreadable, unlike his eyes. As Sadie's gaze locked onto his, she found herself back under the Northern Lights with Martin, side by side, and suspended in a universe of stories yet to be told.

"Sadie?" Martin prompted, pulling her attention back to the present.

"Sorry, I just...I don't know. Felt a little light-headed." She undid her scarf, welcoming the biting air on her skin as her body flashed with heat from the sudden surge of connection. "I'm truly grateful to be sharing this moment with you."

"Me too," Martin agreed, his smile widening.

They basked in the twinkling lights as the townsfolk around them laughed and celebrated. Martin wrapped his arm around her shoulders. His touch was gentle yet firm, and a rush of affection spread through her body at the contact. Sadie allowed herself to be guided by him, following his lead as they walked around the town square.

"Look at that." Martin pointed to a group of children playing in the snow. Their laughter, contagious and pure.

"I've never built a snowman," Sadie admitted.

"I bet you've built many a sandcastle," Martin said.

"I did," Sadie said, remembering long days at the beach with her parents. "Things are so much simpler when you're a kid."

"Who says we can't find some of that childlike wonder now?"

"Are you suggesting we join them?" Sadie raised an eyebrow.

"Why not?" Martin laughed. "Let's enjoy this night like those kids—without a worry in the world."

Under the beauty of the illuminated town square and the strength of Martin's hand in hers, she agreed. "Alright, deal."

As they approached the group of children, Sadie noticed they were struggling to roll the snowball for the base of their snowman. Martin immediately sprang into action.

"Hey, need some help?" Martin called out.

"Yes, sir," one boy replied, and they eagerly passed the snowball over to Martin.

"Watch and learn, kids." He winked at Sadie as he shaped the snowball, expertly molding it into a perfectly round sphere.

Elation spread through her chest as she watched Martin interact with the children. He was a natural with them, his playful spirit and affable demeanor making it impossible not to smile. Martin caught her eye and motioned with his head for her to join them.

"Looks like we need a head," Sadie observed, joining in on the fun.

The children nodded in agreement, and the group set to work on crafting the snowman's head. Sadie helped the children roll the snow into a ball, and then Martin deftly carved out the snowman's features with a stick.

When finished, they all stood back and admired their handiwork. Martin added one last touch by wrapping his scarf around the snowman's neck. The children cheered, then began to roll more snow, leaving Martin and Sadie alone.

"So, how was that?" Martin asked.

"Well, my hands are numb, but I'd say it was worth it," Sadie said, grinning.

Martin's smile grew until it crinkled the corners of his eyes. "I'm so glad. Now, how about we warm you up with some hot chocolate?"

"I thought you'd never ask," Sadie replied, linking her arm through Martin's. "Lead the way."

They purchased two hot cocoas with whipped cream and marshmallows and continued to stroll through the square.

As the night wore on and the crowd dispersed, Martin escorted Sadie back to her cabin. The cold winter air nipped at their cheeks, but neither minded, lost in their shared experience.

"Thank you, Martin," Sadie said as they stood outside her doorstep. "Tonight was...special."

"Thank you for joining me," Martin replied. "I couldn't have imagined a better way to spend the evening."

Sadie grinned. "I can't believe I'm saying this about spending a winter night outside in Alaska, but me neither."

The following morning, the air crackled with energy as Sadie made her way to the Snowflake Sugar Shop.

"Good morning, Mr. Jenkins," she called out to her neighbor and received a friendly, albeit surprised, wave.

One night of holiday fun and the sun shone brighter. Her heart felt lighter. Martin's enthusiasm could energize the entire town square. In his company, Sadie relearned the art of living in the moment, embracing a simpler, more joyful approach reminiscent of the carefree days of childhood. If that wasn't Christmas spirit, she didn't know what was.

She entered the candy store, finding Rosie already hard at work. Sadie walked right up to her. "Okay. You win."

"What do you mean?" asked Rosie, then burst out laughing when she noticed Sadie's expression. "Wait right there."

Rosie ran into the back office and returned with a Santa hat, which she pulled onto Sadie's head. "There you go."

Sadie laughed and examined her appearance in a mirror. "That doesn't look too bad, does it?"

"No, it does not," Rosie replied. "In fact, one might say it suits you."

Chapter 9

A GUST OF ICY wind whipped around Sadie as she pushed open the door to Caleb's general store, sending snowflakes swirling in her wake. She stomped her snow-caked boots on the wooden floorboards and pulled off her gloves, her hair escaping from beneath her Santa hat. As she glanced around the store, her eyes darted from one cozy corner to another, taking in the soft glow of the lanterns adorned with festive wreaths and the nostalgic scent of spiced cider.

"Sadie. How are you?" Caleb called out from behind the counter, a strand of his short black hair falling across his forehead.

"I'm good. Thanks," she replied.

"You're looking awfully festive."

She touched the Santa hat, laughing. "I lost a bet with Rosie. Now I'm wearing this until Christmas."

"Well, it looks good on you," Caleb said, grinning, then leaned against the wooden counter strewn with jars of candy canes and gingerbread cookies. "What brings you here today?"

"I was wondering if the piece of glass for my broken window is ready?"

Caleb nodded. "Of course. Let me check on that for you." He moved to the back of the store, the floorboards creaking with each step.

He quickly returned. "It hasn't arrived yet. The snow's been quite bad a bit south of us, and things are slow to get through," Caleb said. "But I promise it'll be here within the next few days."

Sadie sighed, her shoulders slumped in disappointment. She knew Caleb was doing his best, and she didn't want to make him feel worse than he already did. Instead of dwelling on the setback, she changed the subject.

"Actually, I was wondering if you knew Martin Kringle? He placed a large candy order with us." Despite her growing connection with Martin, there was a touch of mystery about him, and she was eager to learn more. If nothing else, her reality show experience taught her to be careful. Wasn't it wiser to err on the side of caution rather than risk being careless? Especially since she knew firsthand where that could lead.

"Not that well," Caleb replied. "He's come in here once or twice for something small."

"Oh, so he didn't order his supplies through you?" This surprised Sadie. There were no other hardware stores in town.

"No." Caleb's brows knit together as he pondered her inquiry. "You know, I'm not sure where he's getting his supplies. Why do you ask?"

"I don't know. Just curious."

Caleb's face fell slightly, and he let out a soft sigh. "Truth is, if he were to get them from my store, it would certainly help with the financial struggles I've been facing lately."

"Maybe you could reach out to him about it?" Sadie suggested. "I've gotten to know him, and he's a kind and helpful person."

"Perhaps," Caleb agreed, giving her a small smile of appreciation.

From the corner of her eye, Sadie noticed Eleanor Frost, who had been browsing through stacks of ribbon nearby.

Eleanor made her way toward Sadie and Caleb, her every step a deliberate show of self-declared authority. The disapproving furrow of her brow cast a shadow over the rows of neatly stacked canned goods and dry goods lining the shelves of the store.

"Sadie, Caleb." Eleanor's eyes narrowed as they darted between them. "I couldn't help but overhear your little conversation."

Sadie felt her pulse quicken, and she exchanged a worried glance with Caleb. Eleanor's penchant for gossip could wreak havoc in their small town. Gritting her teeth, she forced herself to meet Eleanor's gaze head-on, refusing to back down.

"Is there something you'd like to say, Eleanor?" Sadie asked, her voice surprisingly steady.

Eleanor's lips curled into a thin, disapproving smile as she crossed her arms over her chest. "Well, it seems to me that the two of you are rather concerned with Martin Kringle's affairs. And I can't help but wonder why that is, exactly."

Caleb cleared his throat. "Eleanor, we were just discussing local business."

"That's right," Sadie said. "Isn't that what neighbors do in Mistletoe? Look out for each other?"

"Indeed," Eleanor replied, her tone icy. "But it concerns me that there's more to this than simple neighborly concern."

Sadie's body tensed. This was exactly the sort of thing she had hoped to avoid—a confrontation with Eleanor Frost, the woman who seemed to take pleasure in finding fault in others. Especially her.

"Look, Eleanor," Caleb said, his voice calming and measured. "We're trying to help each other out, that's all."

Eleanor sniffed disdainfully, her eyes still fixed on Sadie. "Well, I suppose we shall see about that, won't we? And you, Caleb, better look out. Doesn't it concern you that we have two newcomers attempting to take over the downtown square? They've been getting quite cozy, let me tell you. And Martin isn't even using you for supplies. Have you maybe thought that he's trying to run you out of business and buy your property?"

Caleb sighed. "And what would be the end goal? All of us merchants do less and less business each year. Why he started his toy store here is beyond me. Beyond logic."

"Exactly my point," Eleanor exclaimed, poking Caleb in the chest with her long, bony finger before turning on her heel and stomping out of the store.

Sadie turned to Caleb, and they both burst out laughing.

When they finally calmed down, Caleb promised to call Sadie as soon as the glass arrived, and then Sadie proceeded to the candy shop. The wind picked up as she stepped outside, sending a chill down her spine. Or was that her growing uneasiness over Eleanor's question?

Had she done it again? Opened herself to someone without learning more about them first? She'd let "he who shall not be named" sweep her off her feet in a series of romantic gestures, even knowing full well they were orchestrated by the reality show. She'd listened to her heart, not her mind, and it had cost her everything. Her friends, her job, her life in Miami.

Martin was only a friend, but still. Was she so desperate for affection that she was making the same mistake twice?

Not knowing if she was being paranoid or cautious, one thing was certain. She would discover why Martin had invested in a toy store in the middle of Alaska.

Chapter 10

T HE NEXT MORNING, A chilling wind whipped through the streets of the small Alaskan town, rattling windows and sending shivers down spines. Sadie pulled her coat tighter around herself as she stood in the town square. Why the town council insisted on an in-person public announcement instead of a text or news release puzzled her. Still, she dutifully gathered with the rest of the community. A sense of unease settled within her. The townsfolk were abuzz with whispers, their eyes darting nervously toward the dark clouds looming on the horizon.

"Storm of the Century, they're sayin'," murmured an old woman next to Sadie, her voice quivering. "Never seen anything like it."

"Neither have I," replied Sadie, her gaze fixed on the foreboding skies. The storm's approach filled her with an inexplicable sense of dread. The wind carried whispers of change, and she could only wonder what that meant.

Suddenly, the doors of the town hall burst open, and Mayor Gregory Evergreen emerged, his regal posture straight and determined. His neatly trimmed mustache bristled with tension as he climbed onto a makeshift stage and raised his hands for silence. The crowd hushed at once, turning their attention to the distinguished-looking man.

"Good citizens of our beloved town," Mayor Evergreen began, his deep voice resonating throughout the square. "As you all know, there is a storm approaching—a storm unlike any we have faced in generations. In light of this imminent danger, I must make a difficult decision for the safety of our community."

The crowd murmured as Sadie watched the mayor intently, noting the worry etched into the lines of his face. She knew how much pride he took in upholding the town's traditions, and she couldn't help but empathize with the burden of responsibility he bore.

"Regrettably," continued Mayor Evergreen, "I must announce the cancellation of this year's Christmas parade, the holiday market, and the Christmas Eve festival. Our priority now must be the safety and well-being of every citizen."

Gasps rippled through the crowd, and a pang of disappointment rippled through Sadie. Not only at the thought of missing out on the festivities she'd hoped to attend with Martin but for the local businesses missing out on all the tourist money.

"Please, return to your homes and prepare as best you can," Mayor Evergreen urged. "Together, we will weather this storm and emerge stronger than ever."

As the townsfolk dispersed, Sadie longed for the warmth and comfort of her little log cabin, yet the fear of weathering this type of storm alone caused her to shiver. She'd grown accustomed to hurricanes and knew exactly what to do. Here, amongst the trees and snow, not so much. And what about the candy order? If she and Rosie couldn't get it done, what about Martin's event, and what would it mean for their growing friendship?

Sadie sent Rosie directly home and closed the shop. As she was leaving, she gave the door a loving tap. "Good luck, my friend."

The wind whipped through the streets, sending snowflakes swirling into a frenzied dance as Sadie trudged back home. The cold seeped into her bones and fueled her fears about the storm. Anxiety gnawed at her chest, making it difficult to breathe.

"Sadie! Wait up!"

Sadie turned to find Martin hurrying toward her. His cheeks were flushed from the biting wind, and his eyes were filled with concern.

"Martin, what are you doing here?" she asked, hoping he heard her over the howling wind.

"I wanted to make sure you're alright," Martin explained, brushing snowflakes from his hair.

"Of course, I'm fine," Sadie snapped, her fear putting her on edge. There existed also that nagging question of Eleanor's. Why did Martin set up a toy store in this small town? But—and this was a big but—here he stood before her, during a storm, to make sure she was okay. He cared about her safety.

Sadie's shoulders slumped. "Actually, no. I'm pretty scared."

"Then let me help you prepare," Martin said. "We both know this isn't an ordinary storm."

She hesitated, then nodded, unable to resist the genuine concern on his face. "Alright. Thanks."

As they entered the cozy warmth of Sadie's cabin, she was grateful for Martin's presence.

"Where do we start?" Sadie asked, noting the anxiety in her voice.

"Do you mind if I look around?"

"Of course not."

Martin opened cupboards and walked around the house, both inside and out, returning promptly. "So, I have a few concerns."

Sadie's heart beat faster. "Okay. Let's hear them."

"Well, there are certain things you need when preparing to hunker down during a storm." He scratched his beard. "Like non-perishable food supplies and bottled water. You also need a stocked first aid kit and flashlights. Maybe a transistor radio in case your phone dies and you don't have a way to charge it. Most likely, the internet will go down. You have a first aid kit, but the batteries in your flashlight are dead. Same for your radio. I didn't see a generator, either. But the biggest problem is your lack of food and water."

Sadie dropped onto a kitchen chair. "So what do I do?"

There was a long silence, and then Martin said, "Why don't you stay at my house during the storm? We're accustomed to this type of weather and are fully prepared."

Sadie hesitated for a moment. Stay at his house? They were still getting to know one another, and she had questions about his business—or had she let Eleanor Frost mess with her head? Probably. That, along with the baggage from *Single to Wed*, made her reluctant to fully trust him. But that sense of connection...that meant something. Besides, Martin's behavior was the polar opposite of her ex-fiancé's.

She took a breath and tried to clear her mind. The thought of being alone during this storm terrified her. It was also stupid. "Thank you. I think that might be a wise decision. I...I'm sorry to put you in this position."

Martin held out his hand, and she took it, allowing him to pull her off the chair and into an embrace. Apparently, Martin Kringle was a hugger. "It's no inconvenience, believe me."

Sadie nodded against his muscular chest. The storm might not be so bad if she could weather it out like this.

Martin pulled out his phone. "I'm texting Nora to let her know you're coming," he said, fingers typing away. He finished and returned the phone to his pocket. "Now go grab whatever you need, and we'll head out."

Sadie picked up on an undertone of urgency despite his broad smile, so she quickly gathered her essentials.

Outside, the snow fell heavily, blanketing the world in white. Martin whistled, and his sleigh appeared as if out of nowhere, this time drawn by two animals.

"These guys are reindeer," Martin said as they waded through the thickening drifts to the sleigh. "They're much better in deep snow."

"If you say so," Sadie said. "Do you own a ranch or what?"

"Something like that," Martin chuckled and loaded Sadie's items into the sleigh, before helping her up and pulling a blanket across their laps. "Ready?"

"As I'll ever be," Sadie said, laughing out loud at the image of them riding a reindeer-drawn sleigh through a winter storm. The scenario read like a scene from a movie.

Martin's house, a beautiful log cabin nestled among tall pines, came into view after what felt like an eternity. The Christmas decorations adorning the exterior created a picturesque setting reminiscent of a scene from a holiday greeting card. Despite her fear of the snowstorm, Sadie felt a twinge of enchantment.

"Wow, Martin. Your home is lovely," she said.

"Thank you. I'm glad you like it," he replied, beaming with pride. "Come on, let's get inside before we turn into icicles."

As they stepped into the welcoming embrace of Martin's home, Sadie marveled at the cozy and festive atmosphere. A decorated Christmas tree greeted them in the foyer like a sentry and must have reached fourteen feet high.

After shedding her outerwear, Martin directed her into the library. The man had a library!

The floor-to-ceiling bookcase, crackling fireplace, and the tantalizing scent of apple cider immediately put her at ease.

"Make yourself at home," Martin said, gesturing to the comfortable-looking armchair near the fire. "I'll just take your bags up to the guest room, then unhook the reindeer. Won't be long."

"Thank you," she replied, settling into the chair with a grateful sigh. She watched the snow fall outside, beautiful now that she sat beside a roaring fire. Safe, cozy, and comfortable, contentment filled every cell of Sadie's body—something she'd not experienced in a very long time. "Now, this is northern living refined," she whispered and closed her eyes.

"Sadie," Martin said, snapping her out of the tranquil moment. "I'd like to introduce you to my grandfather and cousin. They're in the family room." He led her into a bustling room, alive with people, laughter, and conversation. She was taken aback by the sheer number of individuals milling about, each one engaged in various holiday preparations. How had she not heard them from the library?

"Hello again," boomed a jolly, white-bearded man as he approached Sadie, his eyes twinkling with mirth. She immediately recognized him from the candy store. "I'm Martin's grandfather, Kristopher."

"Of course, Kris Kringle. A hard name to forget," Sadie replied, smiling while shaking his hand. "Based on the order Martin placed, I assume your grandkids enjoyed the candy."

Kristopher laughed. "They certainly did, my dear. They certainly did."

"And this is Jack," Martin said, gesturing toward a tall, lanky man with dark hair tucked under a beanie who was busy untangling a string of Christmas lights.

"Hey," Jack greeted, nodding at Sadie before returning to his task.

Sadie smiled at what she thought of as North Pole aesthetic meets urban chic, noting Jack's fitted red hoodie, designer jeans, and a pair of boots that were both stylish and suitable for the snow.

"And this is Ellie, my assistant and good friend. Behind the table, doing goodness knows what, are her two sons, Simon and Erik."

"Nice to meet you," Ellie said.

"And you," Sadie replied, facing a woman in her forties who exuded a sense of gentle authority. She had reddish-brown hair with silver streaks, neatly styled in a bun, and intelligent brown eyes. Her attire was festive, featuring a red velvet dress complemented by a golden belt. A green woolen shawl was draped over one shoulder, adding to her holiday ensemble.

"I'm the only one not dressed for a holiday party," Sadie whispered to Martin. "Even you're wearing something festive."

Martin glanced down at his red and white knit sweater and shrugged. "What can I say? My family enjoys celebrating this time of the year."

That made Sadie gasp. "Are you having a party? Did I interrupt a family event?"

"Oh, no. Nothing like that. Everyone is leaving soon, anyway."

"Isn't it dangerous for them to be out in this storm?"

He laughed, patting her shoulder reassuringly. "Oh, don't worry. They've been through far worse than this. Besides, we're all used to handling challenging weather."

"Really?" she asked, her curiosity piqued. "What do you—"

"Sadie!" Nora called from the family room doorway, her golden-brown hair tied back in a loose ponytail. "Dad said you were coming."

"Hi, Nora."

"I was about to bake some cookies. Would you like to help?"

"I don't really do any baking."

"I'll show you. It's easy, and it will get you out of the Christmas-on-steroids room." She motioned to the chaos.

"Now, Nora," Kristopher called out.

"Kidding, Great-Grandpa. You know I love it too." Nora turned to Sadie and rolled her eyes, making Sadie laugh.

"Sure, Nora. I'd love to."

"Awesome. Follow me."

In the kitchen, Sadie found herself swept up in the delightful process of cookie-making. Nora chatted animatedly as they measured out ingredients, mixed dough, and cut out festive shapes.

"Your house is so lovely," Sadie remarked. "And I've never seen such beautiful decorations."

"Dad always goes all out for Christmas, sometimes a little overboard, but that's okay. It's our family's favorite time of the year."

"So I've been told," Sadie laughed, standing beside Nora as they pressed sprinkles onto cookies, allowing herself to enjoy the moment, let her walls down, and embrace the warmth that radiated from every corner of this magical place.

* * ❄ * *

The cookies were cooling on the counter, their sweet aroma mingling with the scent of pine boughs and cinnamon. Nora scrolled on her phone while Sadie walked around the kitchen. She found herself drawn to the mantel—yes, the Kringle family also had a fireplace in the kitchen—where a beautiful, hand-carved forest scene held a place of honor.

As she studied the intricate details, she felt a presence at her side.

"Ah, you've discovered my pride and joy," Martin said, his eyes shining as he picked up the tiny figure of a moose. "My father carved that for me when I was a boy."

"Your father has incredible talent," Sadie marveled, unable to tear her gaze away from the delicate craftsmanship. "How is it possible your family's not more well known?"

"Well," Martin chuckled, rubbing his neck sheepishly. "I suppose we're somewhat...unco nventional."

Unconventional didn't begin to cover it, Sadie mused, thinking back on the parade of peculiar characters who frequented Martin's home. His grandfather, for instance, possessed an almost otherworldly vitality, while his cousin bore an uncanny resemblance to a mischievous yet incredibly stylish elf.

"Martin," she began, her curiosity bubbling up inside her. The perfect opportunity to ask about his store had presented itself. "I'm curious. You said your family's business was international. If so, why set up a store in Mistletoe? I can't imagine you selling enough to keep your store running, let alone an arm of an international business. The candy store is barely breaking even, and it's the same for Caleb."

Martin leaned his back against the mantel and looked directly at Sadie. "Well, most of our business is delivery. We don't need to set up the stores, but we like to be a part of the community where we live and work. And our family has enjoyed the northern climate for generations."

He ran an online business. Of course! Why hadn't she thought of that instead of foolishly letting Eleanor Frost play on her insecurities? "Interesting," Sadie said after a pause, wondering if he could help her set up an online store for Snowflake Sugar, especially since Rosie had such a large following on social media. How had she or Rosie not thought of this before?

"Glad you think so." Martin flashed her that gap-toothed grin that she found so endearing. "Now, let's join the others in the family room. I believe they're about to start a game of charades."

As they made their way into the lively, laughter-filled room, Sadie felt her heart swell with affection for this enigmatic man who had opened his home, his family, and his life to her.

Chapter 11

T HE RELENTLESS STORM RAGED on for two full days, transforming the once-familiar landscape into a frozen tundra. As the last snowflake fell, Sadie peered out the window of Martin's house, her breath fogging the cold glass. She blinked in disbelief at the thick white blanket that had swallowed their world whole.

"Three feet of snow," she muttered, shaking her head. "Incredible."

"It sure is," admitted Martin, joining her by the window. He wrapped a protective arm around her shoulders, his warmth seeping through her sweater.

"Guess we better start digging out," Nora chimed in, her excitement palpable as she grabbed her coat and gloves.

"Indeed," Martin agreed, his voice full of determination. "Let's get to work."

The group bundled up and ventured outside, armed with shovels and fueled by a sense of camaraderie. The snow was light. Still, each scoop felt like a small victory as they cleared a path from the house to the driveway.

"Whew!" Sadie huffed, wiping sweat from her brow with the back of her gloved hand. "Who needs a gym membership when you've got this?"

"True," laughed Martin. "But there's something magical about this kind of snow." He lifted a handful and blew it gently, creating a glittering cloud that danced around them.

Sadie couldn't help but appreciate his ability to share his childlike wonder over a handful of snow. Martin appreciated the small things around him and, in doing so, began opening Sadie's heart to the simple delights in life. A balm to her weary soul. The laughter, shared stories, and simple joys of companionship in this cabin with Nora and Martin were treasures she hadn't known she needed.

"Are you alright, Sadie?" Martin asked, concern lacing his voice as he noticed her lingering gaze.

"Y-yeah," she stammered, breaking from her reverie. "Just thinking...about everything."

"Everything?" Martin prodded gently.

"Like how I ended up here, in the middle of nowhere, surrounded by people who genuinely seem to care," she admitted, her voice softening. "It's...nice."

"Sometimes the most unexpected things can bring us the happiness we never knew we needed," Martin said.

Sadie nodded, feeling a rush of gratitude for this strange turn of events that had brought her to this place with these people. As they continued to dig, their laughter and chatter filled the air, making the labor feel more like a shared adventure than a chore.

"Almost there!" Nora shouted as the last mound of snow was cleared away, revealing the frozen path beneath.

"Great job, everyone," Martin praised, his smile wide and genuine. "I'm proud of us."

"Me too," agreed Sadie, her heart swelling with growing affection for both Martin and Nora.

A waft of hot cocoa filled the air as Martin, Sadie, and Nora warmed themselves by the fireplace. The fire cast flickering shadows on the walls, creating a cozy atmosphere that brought a sense of peace to the room.

"Would you like some more cocoa, Sadie?" Martin asked, holding up the steaming pot.

"Thank you," she replied, her cheeks rosy from both the cold and his kindness.

"Sadie, what made you decide to move here and work at the candy shop?" Nora suddenly asked.

"Oh," Sadie said, surprised, her fingers tightening around her cup. Moving to Mistletoe was supposed to be a fresh start, with no one knowing about her recent past in Miami. But there was something about Nora's innocent gaze that made her want to open up. Besides, how hypocritical would it be if she, a hater of secrets, continued to hide a big one of her own?

"Before I moved here, I...I was on a reality show," she admitted, biting her lip. "Have you heard of *Single to Wed*?"

"I have," Nora gasped. "What happened?"

"Things didn't end well," Sadie said, trying to keep her voice steady. "I thought they did. Technically, I won, selected in the final episode as the bride-to-be. I got so caught up in the fantasy of it all I convinced myself we were in love." Sadie sighed. "He lived in California, and I lived in Miami. After the big proposal, I thought he'd want me to move to California after the show ended so I could meet his family and start building our future. He convinced me to stay in Miami since we needed to keep things quiet until the show aired."

Sadie stood and walked to the fireplace. The pain and embarrassment from that night caused her chest to ache. "I thought, fair enough. But as Christmas approached, and he hadn't invited me out to meet his family—I know, red flags everywhere—I thought screw it, I'll go surprise him. So, with the help of the network, I flew to California and surprised him at home, all while the cameras were rolling. And, let's just say he wasn't alone."

"That's awful," Nora said.

"It was, and I wish it ended there, but no. Pulling me aside, he told me off, wondering how on earth I thought it was real when it was nothing more than a game and that I should have known better." Sadie resisted the urge to run out of the room. "I was so hurt and humiliated, I snapped. I walked around his apartment, smashing everything I could, and the camera crew captured it all. It aired after the finale, and it was the most watched episode in the show's history." Even after a year, the humiliation stung. "I got fired. My so-called friends ghosted me, and strangers on the street would laugh if they recognized me, or worse, pretend not to see me at all. If he'd only told me, it would have hurt, but my life wouldn't have imploded. And yes, before you say anything, I know that part of it was my fault."

Martin opened his mouth to speak, but Sadie held up her hand to silence him.

She collapsed onto the couch. "So when a lawyer called me to say I'd inherited a store in a town I'd never heard of from a grandmother I never knew I had, I jumped at the chance for a fresh start."

"Wow," Nora said, running over and giving Sadie a hug. "Sometimes people suck."

"Thank you," Sadie replied, finding comfort in Nora's support.

"Sadie, I'm so sorry," Martin added, reaching out to gently squeeze her hand. "You deserve so much better than that."

Sadie's heart swelled with gratitude as she looked at the pair before her. "Thank you both," she whispered, tears glistening in her eyes.

As the fire crackled, Sadie felt a weight lift off her shoulders. The hurt from her past stung a little less. She'd taken a leap of faith, and it felt freeing. Surrounded by the genuine support of Martin and Nora, she shivered with the sensation that she had found a place where she truly belonged.

She caught Martin's eye, and in that moment, something profound shifted within her. Sadie's gaze lingered on Martin's face, tracing the contours of his expression, seeking clues in his earnest eyes. Each line, each subtle shift of his features, seemed to whisper secrets of a future she dared to hope for. Her heart, wrapped in layers of caution and past hurts, began to break free. As she looked into his open, inviting eyes, something unspoken passed between them—a silent understanding, a tender promise. With a hesitant breath that felt like the first step into a new world, Sadie decided to take the risk. She slowly, tentatively placed her fragile, guarded heart into his waiting hands, a silent offering of trust, hope, and the budding possibility of love.

The warmth from the fire danced across their faces, casting shadows on the walls as the room settled into a comfortable silence. Martin could feel the emotional toll that confessing her broken engagement had taken on Sadie. Her slumped shoulders and bowed head were like silent, poignant testaments to her vulnerability.

Yet, their exchanged glance had been a beacon of unspoken understanding, a silent communion that transcended mere words. It was a seismic shift that resonated deep within his heart. It was as if, in that moment, they shared a silent language, a deep, empathetic connection that bridged their souls.

Feeling a surge of bravery and an overwhelming desire to comfort her, Martin gently wrapped an arm around Sadie. The simple act felt monumental, a protective embrace against the harshness of the world and a declaration of his intention to move beyond friendship. When she leaned into him, her head finding solace on his broad shoulder, it was as if a piece of the universe clicked into place. In their closeness, he felt a profound sense of rightness, a calming assurance that, at that moment, all was as it should be in their small corner of the universe.

"Excuse me," Nora chimed in, startling Martin out of his thoughts. "I think I'll go upstairs and read for a while."

"Sure, honey," Martin said, surprised by his daughter's subtle head tilt toward the door, indicating that she wanted to talk in private.

"I need to talk to Nora for a second. I'll be right back," he said to Sadie.

"Sure," Sadie said, curling her feet underneath her.

Martin walked into the hall, finding Nora lingering at the bottom of the staircase, concern etching her young features. "What's going on?"

"Dad, you have to be careful with your Santa secret," she whispered. "Secrets have hurt Sadie."

Martin nodded solemnly, understanding the gravity of her words more than Nora realized. Both of Sadie's parents had kept secrets, and now this awful fellow. No wonder Sadie hated them so much. "I know, sweetheart. I'll be cautious. But telling her is an enormous risk."

"Dad, come on. It's a bigger risk not to. At least think about it," Nora insisted, her serious eyes searching his face.

"I promise." He hugged his daughter tightly, sealing his vow with a tender kiss on her forehead.

As Nora retreated to her room, Martin returned to the couch, resuming his position beside Sadie. They sat in a tranquil silence, enjoying each other's company as the fire continued to burn, casting a warm glow over the scene that unfolded before them. Sadie had opened up because she trusted him. Martin knew that. Was he brave enough to trust her? He longed to but hesitated. He'd never told anyone before, and now his secret loomed over them like a rain cloud. He felt ill.

Martin reluctantly pulled away from Sadie and, with a sigh, rose from the couch and retrieved his heavy winter coat.

"Let's get you home, Sadie," he said softly, offering her a hand up from the couch.

"Oh, okay," she replied, tucking a stubborn strand of hair behind her ear. "I need to get my bag and say goodbye to Nora. I'll just be a minute."

If his words had wounded her, Sadie concealed it masterfully, plunging him deeper into a sea of guilt. He felt a gnawing ache in his chest. Martin needed breathing room, a moment to untangle the web of emotions that ensnared him. Confessing his secret identity as Santa was no trivial matter; it demanded careful thought, a readiness he wasn't sure he possessed. Yet Sadie's presence enveloped him, eclipsing all else. In her vicinity, his mind became a whirlwind of her—her smile, her laugh, the light in her eyes. She was a melody that played on a loop in his heart, leaving no room for anything else, not even the weighty decision that loomed over him.

Underneath the pale moonlight, the world transformed into a frozen wonderland. The sleigh waited nearby, two majestic reindeer harnessed and ready to guide them through the snowy landscape. As they climbed aboard, Sadie marveled at the beauty that surrounded them.

"Everything looks so different after the storm," she mused aloud as they began their journey.

Martin nodded in agreement. "Storms have a way of changing things, don't they?" His words hung in the air between them, laden with unspoken meaning.

The snow crunched beneath the reindeer hooves as they entered town, revealing the extent of the damage the storm had caused. Fallen branches littered the streets, shattered windows gaped open like wounds, and collapsed roofs revealed the heavy burden of the snow that now covered the town.

"Look at all that damage," Sadie said. "I never thought the storm would be this bad."

Martin's features softened, his eyes focused on the destruction before them. "This is going to take a while to clean up."

"Maybe you could use your magic touch," she teased, nudging him playfully with her elbow.

"Magic touch?" Martin asked, hoping his voice sounded normal. "I'm simply an ordinary toymaker, remember?"

"Ordinary toymakers don't have sleighs pulled by reindeer," Sadie replied with a grin. "There's something special about you, Martin Kringle."

Martin's cheeks flushed with warmth, both from the compliment and from the secret he still kept hidden. He longed to tell her the truth, but there existed a delicate balance between trust and secrecy.

"Maybe I'm just lucky," he said, steering their conversation away from dangerous territory. "Or maybe there's something special about this town that brings out the best in people."

"Perhaps," Sadie conceded.

"I hope you don't mind, but I had a couple of guys from my crew come out and shovel your walkway. I figured you wouldn't want to tackle that when you got home."

She gave him a kiss on the cheek. "Thank you, and thank your crew. I'm sure that's the last thing they wanted to do. Just how many people work at your toy store, anyway?"

The sleigh glided to a gentle halt outside Sadie's cabin, now draped in a thick blanket of snow. "Here we are," Martin announced, avoiding her last question, his breath misting in the chilly air as he helped her down from the sleigh.

"Thanks again," Sadie said. "For everything."

Martin heard a pang of sadness in her voice. She didn't want their time together to end, either.

"Anything for you, Sadie," Martin replied softly, tempted to reveal his secret then and there.

But there was no time for Martin to think because suddenly Sadie's lips were pressing against his. The kiss was tender, lingering, and full of unspoken promises. As they pulled apart, he could still feel the ghost of her touch on his lips, a sensation he wanted to savor.

"Goodnight, Martin," she whispered.

"Goodnight, Sadie," he returned, his voice low and filled with emotion.

With a final smile, Sadie turned and walked toward her front door, her boots crunching in the snow. Martin watched as she fumbled with her keys, and when she turned back to wave, his heart beat so loudly he thought he might shake the snow off the roof of her cabin.

"See you soon?" she called out, warming his heart even more than the layers of his winter coat.

"Count on it," he grinned. And with that, his decision was made.

Chapter 12

S ADIE HUMMED CHRISTMAS CAROLS as she approached the Snowflake Sugar Shop. The sight before her caught her off guard, and she immediately stopped humming—the sidewalk leading up to the store had been meticulously shoveled, and the doors were cleared of snow.

As she unlocked the door and entered the store, Rosie's cheerful voice rang out behind her. "Morning, Sadie."

"Morning," Sadie replied, then pulled out the Santa hat from her bag and pulled it on, causing Rosie to laugh. "Don't laugh. A promise is a promise."

"I'm sorry, but you look so darn cute. And boy oh boy, can you believe all this snow?" Rosie asked, gesturing towards the window whcre fat snowflakes began falling, adding to the already impressive accumulation.

"I used to live in Miami, remember, so no, I can't," Sadie said, her gaze fixed on the cleared sidewalk outside. "Hey, Rosie, did you shovel the walk this morning?"

"Me? No. Maybe it was one of our neighbors?" Rosie suggested, her optimism shining through as always. "You know, a little gesture of goodwill during this terrible storm. And it's not only our shop. The sidewalk for the entire square has been shoveled."

"Interesting," Sadie said, pretty certain it was Martin's crew. "Anyway," she continued, changing the subject. "I spent the storm with Martin Kringle and his family." She tried to sound nonchalant, but her cheeks burned a little at the admission.

"Really?" Rosie's eyes sparkled with curiosity. "No wonder you're glowing today. How was it?"

"Oh, you know, fine, I guess," Sadie said with a coy laugh as Rosie rolled her eyes.

Sadie was about to say more, but when she reached for the switch to turn on the twinkling fairy lights that lined the shelves, they remained dark. She then tried the main lights. Still nothing.

"Rosie, did you come back to the store and turn off the power before the storm?" Sadie asked, her brow furrowing in confusion.

"No, I didn't," Rosie replied, concern now etching her features. "Why? What's wrong?"

"The power's off," Sadie said, flicking the switch back and forth in frustration. "And it's freezing in here. I wonder how long it's been off for?"

"I'll check the water," Rosie called out, heading to the sink. "If the pipes have frozen, we're in trouble." She attempted to turn the faucets on. "Son of a gumdrop, they're frozen. This is bad, very bad. I guess the generator stopped working."

"Generator?" Sadie asked.

There was a pause, the silence as cold as the room. Sadie's stomach knotted.

"Rosie, what generator?" she asked again.

"The one beside the back door. Outside in the alley. We always switch to generator power during a storm."

"Well, I didn't know that." Sadie's voice rose an octave as she began to panic. "Our supplies. Our candy. Martin's order."

"The worst thing to do is panic," Rosie said.

"I know, but it's the only thing I can think of doing right now. Martin's counting on us for his order," Sadie said, her voice filled with worry. "Christmas is a huge deal to his family. I don't know what we're going to do."

"Well, the candy we've already made should be fine. I don't think being frozen will hurt it. My mom's frozen truffles before and eaten them at a later date. So, it's really the new candy that's the issue since we can't work here. I don't even know if I should turn on the generator because if any pipes have burst and they thaw, we'll have an even bigger mess," Rosie said.

Sadie sighed, trying to tamp down her rising dread. "Alright. But let me call Martin." Sadie reached for her phone. "He needs to know we might not get everything finished." She opened the screen and immediately noticed a text notification from him she had missed earlier. Opening it, she quickly scanned it and then read aloud, "Sadie, I'm sorry for the short notice, but I had to go out of town for a day or two. I won't be reachable until I return."

"Out of town?" Rosie echoed, a worried frown on her face. "Now what?"

"We're on our own, then." Sadie removed her Santa hat and tossed it on the counter.

"Maybe not entirely," Rosie suggested. "We could call Caleb. He's always been good at fixing things."

"Right, yes, great idea," Sadie agreed, dialing Caleb's number before she even realized it. He picked up after two rings.

"Hey, Sadie," Caleb greeted, his cheerful voice providing a small comfort amid the chaos. "What can I do for you?"

"Hi, Caleb," Sadie replied, trying to sound calm. "We have a bit of a situation here at the store. The power's out, the pipes are frozen, and we have a huge candy order to finish for Martin Kringle. Do you think you could come over and help us?"

"Of course, Sadie," Caleb assured her without hesitation. "I'm not sure what I can do, but I'll be there with my toolbox. Hang tight."

"Thanks, Caleb," Sadie said, relief flooding through her. "See you soon." She hung up the phone and turned to Rosie. "Caleb's on his way with some equipment. Hopefully, that will get us up and running again."

"What a relief," Rosie sighed, pulling her coat tighter. "I don't know how much longer I can stand this cold."

"Me neither," Sadie agreed, rubbing her hands together for warmth. She couldn't help but think about Martin, wondering what could have taken him out of town so suddenly. Her mind raced with possibilities, but she pushed them aside, focusing on the task at hand.

Soon enough, Caleb arrived, his eyes filled with concern. He quickly set to work, examining the pipes at various points in the store.

"Well, there's good news and bad," Caleb announced.

"Don't keep us in suspense," Rosie said while putting a comforting arm around Sadie.

"Well, the good news is that there is only one pipe that has burst. The problem is that I can't find the shut-off valve. You might need the water shut off by the town before I can thaw the pipe and repair it, and I'm not sure how they'd do that under all this snow."

Sadie's hope vanished like air out of a popped balloon, and she felt utterly defeated. "Well, thanks anyway, Caleb."

"Anytime," he replied. "I'm sorry it wasn't better news."

"I know we'll find a way to make this work," Rosie said.

"How?" Sadie retorted.

"We need to think outside the box," Rosie suggested. "Or, more specifically, the candy store."

Sadie hesitated, her skepticism warring with the faintest glimmer of hope. "What we need is Christmas magic," Sadie whispered, reaching for her Santa hat and pulling it onto her head. Standing by the window, she stared at the town square while Martin's words filled her mind: *I suppose it depends on what you mean by magic. I believe in the power of love, the strength of friendship, and the joy that comes from giving to others. If that's magic, then yes, I believe in it wholeheartedly.*

They could do this. They could make the magic they needed. With renewed determination, Sadie nodded. "Alright. Let's see what we've got left and get to work."

"Let me know if I can do anything," Caleb said as he left the store.

"Thanks," Sadie said, then to Rosie, "Okay then, let's get started."

As they sorted through their remaining ingredients, Sadie's thoughts drifted back to Martin, wondering where he was and what was so urgent. She shook her head, returning her attention to the task at hand. They needed a new plan, and they needed it fast.

"Hey, what about using these dark chocolate chips and the peppermint extract?" Rosie suggested, holding up the items triumphantly.

"Peppermint chocolate bark?" Sadie mused aloud. "We can add crushed candy canes for some extra crunch."

"Exactly. It's perfect for the holiday season, and it's something we can make quickly."

"Alright," Sadie agreed, a small smile tugging at her lips. "Now, we need to find somewhere to work."

Sadie's phone buzzed with a text. "Another emergency town meeting," she called out to Rosie. "How come they can text the invite but not the information?"

Rosie laughed. "Mayor Evergreen does enjoy the theatrics."

Sadie gave a nod of agreement, her eyes then drifting toward the window. She observed the townspeople outside, engaged in a flurry of activity as they worked to restore order in the storm's aftermath. She had no doubts about the town's resiliency. You had to be tough to survive in this climate. Yet, as she watched the cleanup efforts, Sadie knew this storm had been so monumental it had somehow reshaped their very destinies.

Chapter 13

S ADIE AND ROSIE FILED into the cramped town hall for the emergency meeting, their winter coats brushing against fellow townspeople as they searched for a spot to stand. The air buzzed with tension, every eye glued to the front where Mayor Evergreen stood tall behind a wooden podium.

"Over there," whispered Rosie, pointing to a sliver of space near Caleb, who had spotted them and waved them over with a concerned smile.

"Sadie, Rosie, I'm glad you made it," Caleb said as they squeezed in beside him. Sadie noticed the worry lines that had etched themselves across his usually cheerful face.

"Thanks, Caleb," she replied. "The mayor sure loves meetings."

Caleb released a small laugh. "This is more than normal, even for Mistletoe."

The murmur of hushed conversations suddenly ceased as Mayor Gregory Evergreen tapped on the microphone, his gaze sweeping the room like a hawk surveying its prey. He cleared his throat, and his deep voice reverberated through the hall.

"Good evening, everyone. Thank you for coming to this emergency town meeting. As you all know, the storm we experienced was nothing short of disastrous." Sadie found her thoughts drifting to her candy store. She clenched her fists as responsibility pressed on her shoulders.

"Unfortunately," Mayor Evergreen continued, "the damage is so extensive that we have no choice but to cancel the rest of this year's holiday festival." A collective gasp echoed through the room, followed by a cacophony of dismayed murmurs. Sadie exchanged worried glances with Rosie and Caleb, knowing how much the festival meant to the town and its economy.

"Canceling the festival will result in a significant loss of revenue for our town," the mayor said, his voice strained. "The consequences of this decision will be felt for months, perhaps even years, to come. Next year will be tough, and I fear that if we cannot find a way to recover, our beloved town might go broke."

"That's not good," whispered Rosie.

How would the town pay its employees, maintain essential services, or meet its financial obligations, such as servicing debt or paying vendors? Services would get cut. Taxes would increase. And more businesses would shut. Possibly the Snowflake Sugar Shop. The thought of one day telling Rosie they needed to close broke Sadie's heart. And what about Caleb? He struggled to make a profit, too. These people, this town, had grown on her. And now, everything was at stake.

"Can't we do something?" Sadie's mind raced as she whispered to Rosie and Caleb. She couldn't bear the thought of this tight-knit community crumbling under financial ruin.

"I don't know what can be done," Caleb said, placing a gentle hand on her shoulder. "But we'll pull through this together, just like we always have."

Sadie wasn't so sure, her chest tightening as she took in the worried faces around her. She had to do something, anything, to help save the struggling town. An idea began to form, and before she got cold feet, she raised her hand, drawing the attention of the room.

"Mayor Evergreen, I have an idea," Sadie said, her voice steady despite her racing heart. "Martin Kringle, the toymaker, placed a large candy order with my store. I'm willing to donate all the profits from the order to start an emergency fund. I know it's nothing compared to the size of a town budget, but maybe it could prevent a business from closing or help pay someone's taxes or keep the lights on for a charity, at least until we solve this problem."

Murmurs rippled through the crowd as they considered her proposal. "The problem is," she continued, "our store was damaged during the snowstorm, and we'll need help to make the candy. If anyone is willing to lend a hand, it could make a big difference for our town."

For a moment, there was only silence. Then Eleanor Frost stood up, eyes narrowing as she fixed her gaze on Sadie. "And why should we trust you?" she asked, her voice dripping with skepticism. "The last time you ran into trouble, you made a fool of yourself—on a reality show, I might add."

Blood pounded in Sadie's ears, drowning out the whispers that ricocheted around the room like stray bullets. She hadn't realized anyone in town knew about her disastrous stint on the reality show, and now she felt exposed and vulnerable. The weight of Eleanor's accusation hung in the air, suffocating her.

"I...I," Sadie stuttered, her confidence evaporating. Her heart sank, and she glanced at Rosie. "Maybe I should go." Her voice was a mere whisper, but it carried with it raw pain.

"Everyone knows about the show," Rosie whispered so that only Sadie could hear. "We've known who you are since you arrived. We do have TV in Alaska, you know." Rosie gave her a small smile.

"You never said anything," Sadie replied in a shaky voice.

"I figured, well, we all figured, you might need some time to recuperate. And you'd bring it up when you were ready. If not, no big deal. And besides, the guy was a jerk. You're better off without him."

Sadie looked Rosie in the eye, and all she saw was friendship and sincerity. She wanted to both laugh and cry as the reality of her situation hit her like a snowball in the face. All this time, they'd known, and all this time, the townspeople were friendly and kind and non-judgemental—except for Eleanor, of course. How this contrasted with the way in which her so-called friends ghosted her after the airing of that disastrous episode. Not a single person supported or comforted her. But here, in this tiny Alaskan town, they'd welcomed her, yet she hadn't seen it. She'd kept her distance, afraid of getting hurt, afraid of not being accepted. She'd been wrong the entire time.

Sadie took Rosie's hand to give her extra strength, then forced herself to meet Eleanor's icy stare. "That's in the past, Eleanor," she said, her tone firm. "I care about this town just as much as anyone else here."

Eleanor raised one disapproving eyebrow. "I don't know about that, but at least you care more than Martin Kringle. I don't see him about tonight. Why should we work to make candy for the likes of him?"

Caleb stepped forward, his face a mixture of determination and support. "Did you miss what Sadie said, Eleanor? She's willing to donate all her profits to the town. That's more than you're doing," he defended, causing several people to gasp and Eleanor's mouth to fall open.

Then another voice rang out.

"The Snowflake Sugar Shop has been a staple of this town for years," Mr. Thompson, the elderly barber shop owner from across the street, declared. "You can't deny the quality of their sweets or the dedication Sadie's put into keeping it afloat."

"Mr. Thompson's right," chimed in Mrs. Baker, the local librarian. "Sadie and Rosie have been working tirelessly to keep the Snowflake Sugar Shop alive."

As more voices joined to support Sadie, their words wrapped around her heart, soothing the sting of Eleanor's cruel remarks.

"Sadie," Caleb whispered, his hand gently touching her shoulder. "As I told you before, don't listen to Eleanor. We all believe in you."

She looked into his warm, brown eyes, and for the first time since arriving in Mistletoe, Sadie knew this was where she belonged. This town was her new home, filled with people whose friendship was worth something. With renewed determination, she turned back toward the crowd, her piercing blue eyes meeting those of her supporters.

"Thank you," Sadie said softly, her voice trembling with gratitude. "I won't let you down."

"Alright then!" exclaimed Mayor Evergreen, his voice ringing out with authority. "Let's not waste any more time. Who here would like to volunteer to help Sadie and Rosie make candy for the emergency fund?"

Hands shot up all around the room, and Sadie blinked back tears of gratitude as she watched her neighbors rally around her. Rosie squeezed her hand tightly, a proud smile on her face.

"Count me in," offered Mr. Thompson. "I've always wanted to try my hand at making candy."

"Me too," piped up young Tommy from the back of the room, his small hand raised high in the air.

"Sadie," whispered Rosie, leaning in close. "We're all in this together."

Sadie nodded, touched by the strength of their support. "Thank you all so much," she said, her voice strong. "It's unlikely our supplier will be able to get through, so we'll need supplies like sugar, milk, and chocolate. Anything you can spare would be greatly appreciated."

"Leave it to us," assured Mrs. Baker, already scribbling a list of supplies on a scrap of paper. "We'll gather everything we need."

"Sadie," said Mayor Evergreen, stepping forward with an encouraging nod. "You may use the town hall as a makeshift candy factory. We'll do this together. As a community."

As the townsfolk chattered excitedly about their newfound roles as candy makers, warmth spread throughout Sadie's body.

"Thank you, Mayor Evergreen," Sadie said, shaking his hand. "I promise I'll do everything I can to help save our town."

Chapter 14

MARTIN STEELED HIMSELF AS he entered the conference room, his heart pounding against his chest. A meeting called this late in the season made him nervous.

"Ah, Martin, there you are," his grandfather exclaimed. "Come, sit down. We need to discuss the construction plans for the new toy factory and village."

Martin nodded and took a seat next to Paul, the head of construction. Paul wore a look of concern on his rugged face, and Martin's uneasiness grew.

"Alright, gentlemen," Martin began. "What seems to be the problem?"

Paul grimaced and hesitated before speaking up. "Well, it appears we've made a miscalculation with the location of the toy factory and village. We cannot build where we initially planned."

"But we've already begun. Can't we adjust our plans?" Martin asked, his mind racing to find a solution. "Surely there must be some way to make it work."

"Unfortunately, no," Paul replied, rubbing the back of his neck. "While the town of Mistletoe received three feet of snow, we received four. Our spot in the secluded valley apparently pulls in its own weather systems. Not only has clearing the snow been a struggle, the hologenerator is drawing excess power to keep up. That means we are losing power in the rest of the site. Our underground power source is weaker than expected, so we cannot both work and run the hologenerator during inclement weather. Should we stay here, we are at risk of being discovered. After further geological analysis, it appears that the only spot that would work in this region is—" Paul stopped and sighed heavily. "Well, the actual town of Mistletoe."

Martin's heart dropped, and he could feel the blood draining from his face. "But we can't do that. Building close to town is too risky. The toy store is already raising questions."

"Exactly," his grandfather chimed in, his voice somber. "We've been protecting our identity and operation for generations. We can't risk exposing ourselves now."

"Then what do we do?" Martin asked, his mind racing with the implications of moving their operation. He longed to stay put, longed for Nora to have stable years as a teenager. And then, of course, there was Sadie. He'd fallen hard.

"Martin," his grandfather said, offering a sympathetic smile. "I know you've grown fond of the town and a certain young lady, but we have no choice."

Martin looked down at his hands; his thoughts of Sadie clouded the decision before him. But he knew they had to move. There was no other way. "Alright," he said, his heart heavy with the burden of their decision. "Let's start researching a new location."

Chapter 15

S ADIE GLANCED AT HER phone. It was nearly six. Martin's earlier text stated he was back in town and hoped she'd join him for dinner. Yes, she'd replied immediately. Now, excitement bubbled inside her as she stepped outside. Delight lit up her face as Martin's sleigh, pulled by two magnificent reindeer, came into view.

"Good evening, Sadie," Martin called out, his grin spreading wide. "Ready for our little adventure?"

"Adventure? Sounds fun," she replied and climbed onto the sleigh, settling beside him as he clicked his tongue and set the reindeer into motion.

"You look beautiful," he said, leaning over and brushing her cheek with a kiss.

She flushed. "You can barely see me under my hat and scarf."

"Your eyes," he said. "They're sparkling, like the unwavering light of Polaris."

Sadie swallowed the emotion that lodged in her throat. "If they are, it's because of you," she whispered.

Martin took the harness in one hand, then intertwined his free hand with Sadie's. "I know we just met, but I feel such a strong connection with you." He pulled her hand toward his lips and brushed it with the gentlest kiss. "I'm probably coming on too strong, but I can't help it. In the boundless expanse of my existence, you have become my North Star, a celestial constant amidst the ever-twirling canvas of my world."

Tears pooled in Sadie's eyes. No one had ever said anything so beautiful to her.

"I'm sorry. I've made things awkward, haven't I?"

"No, not awkward," Sadie replied, leaning her head on his shoulder and squeezing his hand. "But being with you feels too good to be true. Like one day, I will wake up from this beautiful dream and be heartbroken."

"Not if I can help it," Martin replied, his tone surprisingly serious.

Sadie sat up, laughing, and gave him a playful shove. "You're too much, Martin Kringle." When he turned to face her, she grabbed him by the collar and gave him a deep, passionate kiss. She may not have the heart of a poet like Martin did, but at that moment under the velvety night sky, she knew wholeheartedly that Martin was her star too, burning with an unfading glow and illuminating her every step with light and certainty.

As they glided through the snow-covered streets, Sadie couldn't shake the feeling that something extraordinary was happening—not only between her and Martin but also within herself. For the first time in years, she was opening up and letting people in. And oh, how cathartic that was. Expressing to Martin her pain over the secrets her parents had kept loosened their hold on her, and watching the town pull together to help the Snowflake Sugar Shop restored her belief in the goodness of people. Then there were Rosie and Caleb, and the whole town, who stood by her even after her public meltdown on the reality show. This was friendship. This was trust. This was what it meant to be part of a community. She was both terrified and exhilarated. And this awakening, this understanding of belonging, had all begun because of the man by her side.

"I don't know if I ever told you how beautiful the sleigh is," Sadie said, breaking the cocooning silence they'd become enveloped in. She ran her fingers along the intricately carved wooden rails.

"Thank you. I made it myself," Martin replied, a hint of pride in his voice. "It's a Kringle family tradition. Like a coming-of-age type of thing."

"You're not serious?"

"I swear." He placed his hand on his chest.

"Your family is unique, that's for sure," she said, laughing.

"That we are," Martin agreed.

The sleigh came to a gentle halt outside Martin's snow-covered cabin. The warm glow from the windows cast a welcoming light on the frosty ground, inviting them in. Sadie's heart raced with anticipation.

"Ah, here we are," Martin said as he helped her down from the sleigh. "I hope you're hungry."

Inside, the cabin was cozy and charming, with a roaring fire in the hearth and the aroma of freshly baked bread filling the room. The table was set for two, adorned with flickering candles and a bouquet of vibrant red roses.

"Martin, this is...it's beautiful," Sadie said, her voice soft.

"Nothing but the best for you," he replied, pulling out her chair with a flourish. "And it's just the two of us. Nora is helping Ellie prepare for our Christmas Eve event. That night is typically a bit hectic, but I'm hoping, unless you have other plans, that you'll celebrate Christmas Day with us."

"I'd love to," Sadie replied. "What can I bring—and don't say candy." They both laughed.

"Just yourself. We have it all covered."

"You're sure?"

"Absolutely."

They sat and shared a delicious meal, the conversation flowing effortlessly between them.

"Again, I'm sorry for having to take off so suddenly the other day. We had a crisis I needed to deal with," Martin said.

"And everything's worked out?"

Martin shrugged. Something washed across his face then disappeared. "It's handled. Not the best solution, but the only one we could come up with. But enough about work. Tell me what happened in town while I was gone."

"We had a bit of a crisis, too," Sadie exclaimed, her voice rising with excitement. "Have I got a story for you."

"Tell me," he urged.

Sadie explained everything, from the burst pipes to the town hall meeting to the donations of her profits from the candy order.

"That's incredibly generous of you," Martin said, admiration clear in his voice.

"Thanks, but wait until you hear what happened next." She paused for dramatic effect. "Eleanor Frost stood up in front of everyone and questioned my sincerity. Can you believe it?"

"Sadly, I can," he replied with a knowing smile.

"Then she announced how I made a complete fool of myself on that reality show," Sadie continued, her face turning a shade of crimson at the memory. "I thought they'd laugh me out of Mistletoe. Instead, the entire town stood up for me. In fact, they already knew about the show."

Martin's eyes widened in surprise. "Really? That must've felt amazing."

"Unbelievable," she breathed, her chest swelling with pride. "I never thought I'd see the day when Eleanor's gossip backfired on her." Or when I'd be so accepted, she thought.

"I'm really proud of you for standing up to Eleanor and for your generosity toward the town," Martin said. "And while you blame yourself for what happened after that show—"

Sadie cut him off. "It's okay. Thanks to your support and the support of the town, I'm figuring things out, and I've realized that no one knows how they're going to react in a situation like that. I reacted by smashing a few wine glasses and a vase. Not my proudest moment, but I'm a little bit wiser now and it's time to move forward. And you know what? I think everything's going to be okay."

"I hope so too," Martin said, his tone serious again. He took a sip of water. "I have something for you."

"Really?" she asked, curious about what could elicit such a change in his demeanor.

"Close your eyes," he instructed, and she complied, feeling a mix of excitement and trepidation. Why was Martin so serious?

When she opened them again, Martin held a small wooden box in his hands. It was intricately carved with delicate patterns, its aged wood polished to a rich sheen. She took it from him, marveling at the craftsmanship.

"Go ahead, open it," he encouraged.

As she did, the tiny box unfolded, as if by magic, into an elaborate, magnificent music box. Tiny figures danced and twirled as a hauntingly beautiful melody began to play, echoing throughout the room. Sadie stared in wonder, her eyes wide with astonishment.

"Martin," she breathed. "It's...it's incredible. How is this even possible?"

"That's what I want to tell you."

Sadie furrowed her brow, trying to decipher the meaning behind his words.

He paused momentarily, as if preparing himself for what he was about to say, making Sadie's stomach tense up.

"There's no easy way to say this, so I'm just going to say it." He took a breath. "I'm Santa Claus."

"Excuse me?" she snorted, her face contorting into a mixture of disbelief and annoyance.

The romantic atmosphere dissolved instantly, replaced by a palpable tension.

"Santa Claus," he reiterated calmly, as if the words were the most natural thing in the world. "I know it sounds preposterous, but it's true."

"You expect me to believe that you, Martin Kringle, are actually Santa Claus?" she scoffed, standing so quickly her chair tipped over. She ignored it, crossing her arms defensively and staring down at Martin. "I knew it was too good to be true. Did you enjoy playing me for a fool?"

Martin stood and faced her. "Of course not," he replied, reaching for her hand, but she stepped back. "I would never mock you, Sadie. All I want is for you to know the truth."

"The truth that you're Santa Claus? That's absurd!"

"Sadie, please," he implored, his eyes pleading with her to give him a chance to explain. "Think about it. How does the music box work, if not by magic? Why do I have a sleigh? My last name is Kringle, for Pete's sake."

She hesitated, recalling the enchanting music box, the sleigh rides through the snow, the mysterious donation of Christmas lights to the town, his grandfather named Kris Kringle, Martin's kind heart, and the undeniable affection she felt for this man. But admitting that Martin was the embodiment of a magical, mythical being seemed like a bridge too far.

"Even if there is more to you," she said, her voice wavering, "that doesn't mean I can accept this...this fantasy of yours."

"All I ask is for you to keep an open mind," he replied, his expression softening. "There are things in this world that defy explanation."

Sadie's heart raced as she weighed his words against her own beliefs. Could it be possible? Could the magic she had witnessed tonight—and the inexplicable connection she felt with Martin—be evidence of something...unknown?

She sighed. "I'm not sure. I want to believe you, I honestly do, but you seriously can't expect me to take your word for something so fantastical."

"I can prove it," he blurted. "And I swear to you, on the magic of Christmas itself, that I am telling the truth." Martin's voice was so sincere that she allowed him to take her hands in his. "Let me prove to you I'm Santa Claus."

As his words slowly sank in, Sadie found herself questioning everything she knew, or thought she knew, about the world around her. The once-grumpy skeptic now faced an impossible choice: to embrace the magic that had eluded her for so long or to cling stubbornly to her old beliefs.

Did even thinking that mean she was becoming entangled in his delusion? There was only one way to find out.

"Alright," she said. "Prove it."

Martin's gloved hand extended toward Sadie, offering assistance as she climbed back into the sleigh. The worn leather creaked under her weight, and she pulled a blanket around her.

"Are you ready?" Martin asked.

Sadie nodded. She couldn't shake the feeling that she'd always known there was something different about him, but Santa Claus? No way.

As the sleigh carried them further out of town, Sadie retrieved her phone from her pocket and typed out a quick message to Rosie.

"Having dinner with Martin." She hit send. Immediately, she received a reply of three heart emojis.

"Everything alright?" Martin asked, concern in his eyes.

"Um, yeah. Just letting Rosie know where I am," Sadie replied. "That way, if I'm never seen again, they'll know where to begin the search."

"Ah, good idea," he chuckled.

They traveled in silence, the rhythmic sound of the sleigh gliding over snow its own form of conversation. Sadie found herself questioning everything she knew about this man. If he really was Santa Claus, why would he reveal himself to her? And if he wasn't, then she was in big, big trouble.

Her thoughts swirled like snowflakes in the winter wind as they journeyed further into the forest. Sadie felt a strange mixture of anxiety and anticipation building within her chest. What awaited her beyond the familiar streets and storefronts? And more importantly, could she trust the man guiding her there?

The snowflakes danced around them as the sleigh continued its journey, the reindeer's breaths puffing out in small clouds of condensation. Sadie shivered, drawing the blanket even tighter. The silence between them was thick as Martin's revelation hung heavily in the air.

She stole a glance at him, taking in his confident posture and the way he guided the sleigh with ease. He appeared unfazed by their quietude, but was it all an act?

"Sadie," Martin finally said, breaking the silence. "I know this must be difficult for you to understand, and it means everything to me that you'd trust me enough to listen, so let me explain everything."

She turned to face him fully. "Go on," she prompted.

"So the magic in my family goes back generations. Currently, my grandfather Kris is the one in charge, the CEO, if you will," he began, his voice steady. "My father and aunt, they're like vice presidents. They help oversee the entire operation."

"And you?" Sadie asked, searching his eyes for any hint of deception.

"Me? I'm more like a general manager," Martin said, a wistful smile tugging at the corners of his lips. "All the Santa Clauses are."

"Wait. What do you mean all?"

"This is where reality and legend differ. My cousins and I work together to manage toy production and delivery. There's not only one Santa Claus. It's way too big a job for one person. Currently, there are eight of us."

Sadie's head hurt as she tried to reconcile Martin's version with what she'd believed as a child. Then she remembered Martin's grandfather requesting candy for his eight grandchildren and how Martin described his toy business as an international conglomerate. "Eight?"

"Correct. We're spread across the world and run things on the ground."

"Sounds more like a crime syndicate," Sadie said, causing Martin to laugh.

There was something about the sincerity in his voice that made her want to believe him, but the rational part of her mind kept whispering that it was impossible.

"Why are you telling me all of this?" she asked.

"Because in order for our relationship to go any further, I need you to understand who I am. And not only that, I want to be open and truthful, as you've been hurt by secrets before. Especially at Christmas."

Sadie stared at him, searching for any hint of falsehood. The idea of him being part of the legendary Santa Claus family was still hard to swallow. That she even referred to it as the 'legendary Santa Claus family' was comical. But as she studied his face, he held only sincerity and unwavering determination in his gaze, and the smallest, teeny tiniest part of her heart started to believe.

Sadie swallowed hard, her heart pounding. She had so many questions, but she didn't know where to begin. All she could do was hold on to the sides of the sleigh and brace herself for whatever lay ahead.

Eventually, the sleigh came to a halt near a clearing at the edge of a wild forest. Snow-covered trees towered above them, their branches drooping. A sense of calm settled over the scene like a blanket, muffling the sound of their breaths in the crisp air.

"Take my hand," Martin said, reaching out to her.

Sadie hesitated only briefly before placing her gloved hand in his.

"Now, close your eyes," he instructed gently. "This might feel a little weird, and sometimes it stings."

"Stings? What stings?"

"Going through the force field."

"The what?"

"It will all make sense in a minute. You've come this far. Please humor me a bit longer."

She clung to Martin's hand like a lifeline, willing herself to have faith in the extraordinary. She thought of his smile, his laugh, his poetic heart, his welcoming family, of Rosie and Caleb, of the town supporting her, and of how much her life had changed since moving to Mistletoe. Martin had shown her that the spirit of Christmas was about the joy of connection, the beauty of kindness, and the warmth of shared humanity.

That was the true magic of the season, and since she'd already accepted that, perhaps she could also believe in another type of magic.

"Okay. Let's do this," Sadie said with a nod and squeezed her eyes shut, feeling silly and vulnerable all at once. Somehow, Sadie knew her life was about to change forever. So, she drew in a deep breath, filling her lungs with cold, invigorating air, and embraced the possibility of the impossible.

"Here we go," Martin whispered, and a tingling wave surged through her body.

"Okay, open your eyes," Martin said, his breath warm against her cheek.

As her eyelids fluttered open, her breath caught in her throat. The forest had transformed into a bustling construction site, with people working on tearing down buildings and dismantling structures. The air was thick with dust, and the sound of hammers and saws echoed all around.

"What—what is this?" she stammered, her heart hammering.

"Santa's Village, where we make the toys and where my team lives. Or at least it was going to be."

"What? Why?"

"Every story has its share of challenges," Martin said softly, his grip on her hand tight with reassurance. "Ours is no different."

"Challenges? I don't understand," she admitted, unable to tear her gaze from the chaotic scene before them.

"Come with me," Martin said, and together they disembarked the sleigh and walked closer to the village. "You see that shimmer over there?" he asked, pointing toward a faint, iridescent glow that encircled the entire area.

Sadie squinted, trying to focus on the barely perceptible light. "Yes, I think so."

"That's our power source," he explained. "But it's been struggling lately. There isn't as much power in this valley as we expected."

A chill ran down Sadie's spine as the gravity of the situation sank in. Her gaze darted between the workers and the power source, her mind full of questions. She watched the scene for a long time before asking, "So, how does this all work? Are those people elves?"

"No, no, that's all legend," Martin said. "You met Ellie. She's not an elf."

"Well, I guess she didn't quite match my expectations of an elf's appearance. Then again, you don't look like Santa."

"True enough, I suppose, but I will when my hair turns white," Martin replied. "The people you see are families that have worked for mine for generations. They're regular people who work for a magical family."

"So, like indentured servants?"

"Oh, goodness, no. Nor is it some kind of labor camp. Anyone can change locations, change jobs, or even leave."

"Leave? Won't they reveal your secret?"

"Not typically, although it has happened. But even when it does, it's not believed."

"And yet you expect me to believe you?"

"Yes, because I'm showing you proof. Those who have spoken out have only had their word."

"Did your family hunt them down and silence them?"

"Again, we're not organized crime."

"Still, this is a lot," Sadie said, turning toward the sleigh. Martin nodded and followed her lead, leaving behind the magical village, a sight that left Sadie overwhelmed. She pulled her coat tighter around her, trying to shield herself from the icy bite of reality—how did a fictional tale become a reality?

Sadie's gaze followed the workers as they dismantled what seemed to be a workshop, her mind still reeling from the revelation. She glanced over at Martin, who was watching the scene with a somber expression. "So, if there's not enough power, what happens next?" she asked.

Martin sighed, his eyes never leaving the bustling activity before them. "We have no choice but to move our operation to another location, far away from here."

"Move?" Sadie echoed, trying to wrap her head around the idea. "But you can't go. You just moved here."

"I know," he admitted, sadness lacing his voice. "But we can't risk exposing our secret to the world. The magic needs to be protected, and if that means uprooting our lives and starting anew, then so be it. We have to do what's for the greater good."

Sadie chewed on her lower lip. Despite the magical world that had been revealed to her, her thoughts focused on one thing: Martin was leaving.

"Can you please take me home?" Sadie asked. "This has been a lot to process."

"Of course," he replied. "I understand."

The sleigh penetrated the force field again, and the same tingling sensation washed over Sadie before the noisy world of the village fell into silence and disappeared without a trace.

"I've been thinking," she said hesitantly, her eyes locked onto a point far away. "If you have this magic, this power...could you use it to save Mistletoe?"

Martin sighed. "It's not that simple. Christmas magic is powerful, yes, but it can't solve the world's problems. Its purpose is to kindle hope and joy in people's hearts, but ultimately, the fate of a town like Mistletoe lies in the hands of its residents."

"Then what's the point?" Sadie retorted. "If your magic can't help people in need, then why even have it?"

"The world is a complex place, filled with both beauty and hardship. My magic can't fix everything, but it can inspire people to come together and create positive change in their own lives. You're a perfect example of that."

"Me?"

"Yes. The way you offered your profits to help the town. That's Christmas magic."

Her breath hitched as she considered Martin's words, but she fell into silence and stared out at the dark landscape.

As they approached her small, snow-covered cabin, Sadie watched the familiar sight come into view, her heart heavy with uncertainty. The street was lined with festive decorations, but now they mocked her rather than fill her with holiday cheer.

"Here we are," Martin announced, pulling the sleigh to a stop in front of her home. He turned to face her, his smile replaced by a look of tender concern.

"Thank you," Sadie whispered, but before she could step out of the sleigh, Martin leaned in and pressed his lips against hers. It was a gentle kiss, but it sent a shiver rippling through her body and made tears spring to her eyes.

"Why did you tell me all this if you're leaving?" she asked, her voice barely audible as the warm tears ran down her cold cheeks.

"Because I want you to come with me," Martin answered.

Chapter 16

SADIE ROSE EARLY, NOT having slept a wink. How could she when Santa's existence had been revealed? Life would never be the same again. And, on top of that, Santa—make that *a* Santa—wanted her, Sadie Wexford, to join him. She pinched herself hard. *Ouch.* Yup, she was definitely not dreaming.

So now what? She wasn't ready to leave Mistletoe. Nor was she ready to say goodbye to Martin.

"Maybe a walk will help clear my head," she muttered while throwing off the blankets and duvet. She dressed and headed out without breakfast, the winter sun low in the sky and not a cloud to be seen. Her boots sank in the snow as she walked the quiet streets of Mistletoe, immersed in thought.

"Sadie!" Rosie's voice echoed from the street, jolting her to attention. Rosie was crossing from the candy store toward the town square and waving energetically at her. "Come over here."

Following Rosie's lead into the town hall, Sadie pushed open the heavy wooden doors and stepped inside. To her astonishment, the hall had been transformed into a buzzing candy-making assembly line. Rosie now stood at the center of it all, her bright green eyes excited and her red curls bouncing as she managed the steaming pot of hot sugar on the stove.

"How did you organize this so fast?" Sadie asked, scanning the room. Volunteers from the town were dipping, wrapping, and packaging candies at lightning speed.

"Isn't it amazing? Caleb and I set it up last night." Rosie beamed, stirring the hot sugar with practiced ease. "We'll have no problem fill-ing Martin's order now. Your idea worked."

"Really?" Sadie couldn't hide her surprise. People often supported an idea in theory but weren't willing to partake in making it a reality. But not here. Not in Mistletoe.

"Absolutely," Rosie assured her. "You should be proud, Sadie. Your passion for the Snowflake Sugar Shop and Mistletoe has everyone in-spired. Caleb's donating the proceeds from all the Christmas Trees he sells, and Mr. Thomp-son is donating all his profits from haircuts on Saturday."

"I can't believe it," Sadie murmured, her voice barely audible over the clatter of candy making. "And thank you, everyone. I don't know what to say," she said, loud enough for all to hear.

"Say you'll help us finish up," a volunteer called out. The others chuckled and nodded in agree-ment.

"Alright," Sadie agreed, rolling up her sleeves. "I will. Rosie, what do you want me to do?" And as she immersed herself in the whirlwind of candy production, guided by Rosie's unwavering optimism, Sadie knew this town was home.

If only Martin wasn't making her choose between home and love.

"Sadie, where's your Santa hat? A bet's a bet," Rosie called out.

"I forgot it. I'll get it later." Sadie forced a smile. Could she ever wear one again? Did Martin wear one? There were too many questions.

"I'll hold you to that. Now pass me that tray of caramels," Rosie said, her hands and apron coated in sugar. Sadie quickly obliged, her own fingers becoming sticky with the remnants of chocolate and caramel.

"Got it," Sadie grunted, sliding the tray across the counter, happy for the change of topic.

Volunteers bustled around them, their laughter and chatter filling the room. They were like a well-oiled machine working tirelessly.

Soon, the sounds of Christmas carols filled the hall as everyone sang their favorite songs. Everyone but Sadie. Every song about Santa caused her chest to tighten and her stomach to knot.

"Sadie?" Rosie's voice interrupted her thoughts. "You've been awfully quiet. What's on your mind?"

"Nothing," Sadie lied, trying to keep her emotions in check.

"Come on, spill it," Rosie insisted, a knowing glint in her eye. "I can tell something's bothering you."

"Alright," Sadie sighed, deciding to confide in the colleague she now knew was also her friend. "Martin told me he's leaving Mistletoe."

"He's leaving? Why? When?"

"Apparently, there's some building code issue or something." How did Martin keep up the rouse? She was struggling the first time she tried. "And I'm not sure exactly when he's leaving, but I think it's as soon as possible."

"What about the candy order?"

Sadie froze. The candy order. He wouldn't cancel it, would he? She pulled out her phone and texted Martin.

We need to talk. ASAP.

It buzzed back right away.

This is Nora. Dad forgot his phone. Again.
Will he be home soon?
I think so.
Good. I'm heading over.
Wait. I'll send the sleigh. It's easier that way.

Sadie was about to type no thank you. Then she realized she had no idea how to get to Martin's cabin.

Okay. I'll wait in front of the candy store.

"I'll be back soon," she said to Rosie. "Hopefully, with some answers."

Chapter 17

S ADIE RAISED HER HAND, rapping on the door of Martin's cabin.

"Come in. It's open," called Nora's cheery voice from inside. Sadie turned the knob and stepped into the cabin. Nora stood by the fireplace, her golden-brown hair reflecting the flickering flames like a halo around her head. Her big, curious eyes danced in the firelight as she smiled at Sadie.

"Hi, Sadie. Dad's away on business, but he'll be back soon." Nora motioned for Sadie to take off her coat and hang it on the coat rack near the door. "Make yourself comfortable."

"Thanks," Sadie replied, her voice tense as she peeled off her gloves and took a seat on one of the plush armchairs facing the fireplace. She glanced around the cabin, her eyes lingering on the carefully carved forest scene that adorned the mantel. Beside it sat the music box Martin had given her, forgotten here before their sleigh ride.

She walked across the room and held the smooth box in her hands, reluctant to open it and watch the magic unfold.

"Can I offer you something to drink? Hot cocoa, maybe? Or tea?" Nora asked, breaking the silence.

"Sure, tea would be great," Sadie replied. There was an uneasiness settling in her stomach. Nora returned shortly with a tray of tea. Sadie watched as the steam danced above the mug, then took a deep breath.

"Listen, Nora...there's something I need to talk to you about," she began, her voice wavering slightly. "It's about your father."

"Uh oh, what did he do?" Nora asked.

"He...he..." Sadie hesitated, wondering how to broach the subject delicately, then realized she was fretting over nothing. Nora knew. It wasn't a secret here. "I know that he's Santa. One of the Santas," she corrected.

For a moment, the room fell silent, save for the crackling of the fire. Nora blinked in surprise, then released an enormous sigh. "I'm glad to hear that."

"It's a lot to take in, you know?"

"I can imagine," Nora agreed, her eyes filled with empathy.

"I never thought something like this could be real." Sadie glanced around the cozy cabin, taking in the festive decorations as if they corroborated Martin's identity.

"Yeah, but you get used to it. You'll find it pretty normal soon."

"Well, except that you're moving," Sadie began, then checked the time on her phone. Rosie was expecting to hear from her. Maybe there wasn't time to wait for Martin. "I don't know how much your dad shares with you about...the business…but with everything that's happened, I'm worried he's going to cancel the order at the candy store."

"Oh, of course not. He still has to include the candy with all the gifts on Christmas Eve. Nothing's changed there. The village is being moved. That's all. It's happened before. No biggy. It's not like Christmas is being canceled."

"Are you sure?" Sadie asked. "About the candy—not Christmas—oh, you know what I mean. This is hard."

"Absolutely," Nora replied with conviction. "My dad wouldn't do that."

"Well, that's good to hear. I'm going to let Rosie know the order is still on and then head out." Sadie texted Rosie the good news. "And don't worry, your secret is safe with me."

"You're not waiting for Dad? I know he'd want to see you."

Sadie's chest ached with conflicting emotions. "Not just yet. I still need time to think." She cared for Martin, but leaving Mistletoe would mean abandoning the place that had become home.

"About dating Dad? The Santa Claus thing?"

"About leaving Mistletoe."

"Him leaving?"

"No, me."

"Why would you leave?" Nora asked.

"Because he asked me to go with him."

"Are you kidding? You guys just met." Nora facepalmed, then stood. "I'm sorry, Sadie. He never dated after Mom died and is obviously a bit out of practice. Don't let that scare you off, though. He really is a good guy."

"I think so too. That's why this decision is so hard."

"Maybe," Nora suggested, "you could consider a long-distance relationship? I mean, once Dad's busy season is over, it's easy for him to travel."

Sadie blinked in surprise, Nora's suggestion catching her off guard. But as she mulled it over, she couldn't deny the spark of hope it ignited within her. Unfortunately, fear soon followed. "I don't know. My last long-distance relationship ended in disaster."

"Because of that jerk on *Single to Wed*?"

Sadie nodded.

"Did you ever watch the entire show?"

"No," Sadie admitted.

"I did. I streamed the entire season after you told us what happened. And he played you from the start. Don't feel bad that you lost your temper. He deserved it. And please don't think that my dad is anything like that guy."

Sadie closed her eyes and ran her fingers across the music box. Everything Nora said was true. Martin was one in a million. He'd never hurt her or anyone the way Todd—wait. She'd used his name without feeling sick or ashamed. The hurt remained but as part of her past. Not something that tainted her daily life. She felt so free.

"You're right, Nora," Sadie said, her strength and conviction growing by the second. "You're absolutely right. We could make it work for now. And then, in the future, who knows?"

"Exactly," Nora exclaimed. "Now we just have to tell Dad." She got up and put another log on the fire. "You know, it's kind of ironic that the place with the best power source for the toy factory is Mistletoe itself."

"Wait. What?" Sadie asked.

"The power source we need is at its strongest under the town. Not where we set up the plant. I guess there was a miscalculation."

"Would it hurt the town if the plant used this energy source?"

"Oh no. They'd never know. We just have to be close. It's not like electricity. It can't travel far."

A heavy quietness settled over the room, weighing down on Sadie's chest like her weighted blanket. She chewed on her bottom lip. Then, as if struck by lightning, an idea sparked within her, so incredible and daring that it left her momentarily breathless.

"Wait a minute," she exclaimed, sitting up straighter in her chair. "Why not incorporate it into Mistletoe? We could move the village there and keep the town alive."

Nora's eyebrows shot up, her eyes widening with surprise. "You mean...combine the two worlds in Mistletoe?

"Exactly," Sadie said, her heart pounding with exhilaration.

"But we can't have that many people know our secret."

"They wouldn't have to. Essentially, Santa's Village is a company town. Your crew lives near the factory with services to support them. Nothing suspicious there. Also, they are regular people, not elves. Again, no mystery. All we'd have to do is keep the power source hidden, and I'm sure that your people could figure it out, assuming they haven't already. After all, you were building a village, and no one knew. Think about it. The entire town could be Christmas-themed. We could build a theme park and specialized Christmas stores and hold a weekly parade, creating a place where people who love Christmas would want to come, not only during the holidays but all year round." Sadie paused. "It's been done before, of course, but ours would be the best because, heck, it's the real thing."

"Wow," Nora breathed, her eyes shining with excitement. "That's an amazing idea. But do you think Dad, Great-Grandfather, and the other Santas would go for it?"

Sadie hesitated, uncertainty gnawing at the edges of her newfound conviction. But she couldn't let fear hold her back—not when there was a chance to save Mistletoe and keep Martin close by.

"Only one way to find out," she said.

Chapter 18

THE DOOR TO MARTIN'S cabin creaked open, revealing the cozy interior lit by the warmth of a flickering fireplace. His smile broadened as he spotted Sadie sitting in his worn-out leather armchair. He'd worried that he might never see her again after his impulsive invitation. Maybe he hadn't completely scared her off.

"Sadie, I'm so glad you're here," he said, his voice revealing exhaustion beneath his excitement. His robust build sagged under an invisible weight, and he knew his eyes had dark circles underneath.

"Dad, you look terrible," Nora said.

"Why, thank you, sweetie," Martin replied, planting a kiss atop his daughter's head. "But it's nothing that a good night's sleep won't fix." And maybe the news that Sadie was willing to give him another chance. That would help. A lot.

Martin sank into the sofa opposite Sadie, the cushions molding around his weary form. He rubbed his temples, trying to chase away the stress-induced throbbing behind his eyes. "Finding a suitable location has been quite the ordeal. It's taken a toll on me, I must admit, especially with Christmas a few days away and having to use the other sites for all our toys. Everyone is simply exhausted."

"So maybe this isn't the best time to bring this up, but what the heck were you thinking, asking Sadie to move with us?" Nora asked.

Martin's mouth fell open, and he looked at Sadie, who shrugged.

"Dad, you've only known her a few weeks. Way to freak her out. Haven't you ever heard of Facetime? Or if that fails, your magical sleigh?"

"Nora—"

"No, Dad, seriously. I like Sadie, and there you are, scaring her off. Good thing you have me for damage control."

"Damage control?" Had he blown it?

"Yeah. And good thing your girlfriend here is an out-of-the-box thinker. She's come up with an amazing idea to keep the village here."

"She has?" He turned to Sadie. "You have?"

"We think so," Sadie said, with Nora beside her, nodding in encouragement. "So here it is: you move the village to Mistletoe."

The room fell silent as Martin's eyes widened at the suggestion. He hesitated, unsure of how to respond to their well-intentioned plan.

"Move the factory to Mistletoe," he repeated, his mind churning with doubts. "That's quite a bold idea."

"Think about it," Sadie urged. "With your power source under the town, it makes practical sense."

"I don't understand. We can't have all those people leave town. It's their home. I thought you wanted to save it?"

"What? No," Sadie said. "That's not what we mean."

Nora rolled her eyes. "We simply integrate our village into the town."

"You're not serious. It's not that simple," Martin said. Or was it?

Sadie paced in front of the fire. "First, we approach the mayor and city council with the proposal to move your toy factory and staff housing to Mistletoe. Then, we suggest that Mistletoe keeps the Christmas Festival running all year. I'm talking about perpetual garlands and twinkling lights, craft booths, a Christmas tree in the town square, parades, and an amusement park. The elk and reindeer can live in plain sight, maybe like a petting zoo. And then there's the economic boom from all the new housing for your staff. As you said, they're not elves, and Nora told me your team can secretly access the power source. Think of it as turning Mistletoe into a company town. It just happens that the company is Santa Inc." Sadie stopped pacing and faced Martin. "It will be a huge draw for those who seek the joy of the holidays regardless of the calendar. Mistletoe will be saved, and you won't have to move."

Sadie continued, her voice soft yet persuasive. "Instead of hiding Santa's Village, Mistletoe could be a beacon of Christmas spirit, a place where the joy of Christmas never fades, not even in the heat of July."

Martin walked to the window, watching the snowfall. Could it be that easy? Integrating the village with Mistletoe. "You speak of dreams that twinkle like stars."

Nora made a gagging noise. "Please don't tell me he always speaks to you like that, Sadie."

"Watch it, kid," Martin said jokingly, while a blush that rivaled Rudolph's nose spread across his cheeks.

"Let me just say this, and I'll leave you two lovebirds alone," Nora said, turning to her father. "You've dedicated your life to spreading happiness, Dad. Take this opportunity to enjoy some of your own." And with that, Nora ran upstairs, leaving Martin wondering how he was lucky enough to have a daughter like her.

Then he turned to Sadie, catching the hope emanating from her and making his heart beat a little faster. This town, with its perpetual Christmas spirit, could indeed be the perfect backdrop for a new chapter...one where the magic included a touch of love.

He let out a laugh that nearly shook the garland off the walls. "How can I say no? I think that's the best idea I've heard in a long time," he said, and suddenly, Sadie was in his arms. He held her close and silently vowed to never let her go.

Martin's fatigue vanished. Excitement charged the air as they discussed the merging of their worlds and their lives. As the night wore on, a shared vision for Mistletoe was born, woven with the promise of love and the timeless magic of Christmas. Their dreams and their

hearts intertwining like the ribbons on a Christmas gift.

Epilogue

MAYOR EVERGREEN, DONNING A festive holiday-themed suit, tapped on the microphone to gather everyone's attention.

"Good evening," he said. "I'd like to welcome you all to the ribbon-cutting ceremony of the new and improved Mistletoe Village. A place where the holiday spirit never ends."

After the cheers died down, Mayor Evergreen continued. "It's hard to believe that it was only six months ago when Martin Kringle and

Sadie Wexford—let's have a hand for Martin and Sadie."

The crowd clapped until the mayor held up his hands. "As I was saying, it's hard to believe it was only six months ago that these two approached me with their idea. If Martin brought his entire factory here, not just the toy store, it could be the center of something, well, something magical. And now, here we are, ready for opening day. But before we cut the ribbon, I'd like to have Martin come up here and say a few words."

Sadie squeezed Martin's hand. "Good luck," she whispered. As he walked away, Sadie turned to Nora. "You're going to love this."

"Oh, no," Nora said, covering her face with her hands.

"Good evening, ladies and gentlemen," Martin began. "I want to thank the town council and all those who made this project possible, but especially my daughter Nora and Sadie, my fiancee, for being the ones who developed this idea. Ladies, I don't know where I'd be without you." Martin looked at them and winked.

"Tell me it's over," Nora whispered.

"Hang in there. He's just getting warmed up," Sadie said.

"As a toymaker," Martin continued, "Christmas has always been a special time of year, but Christmas is about so much more than toys and presents, because beneath the gentle cascade of snowflakes and amidst the soft glow of twinkling lights, Christmas weaves a spell that awakens the heart's deepest yearnings. It's not just the cold that draws us closer, but the hope and joy that Christmas kindles, reminding us of life's endless possibilities. This season holds a magic that transcends the ordinary, turning fleeting moments into timeless memories. For those who believe in Christmas magic, hope and joy become the heartbeat of every embrace, a silent promise that, despite the world's uncertainties, there remains a steadfast warmth and brightness, waiting to be rekindled each year. In this magical time, the spirit of Christmas becomes the compass guiding us through winter's chill, ensuring that no heart feels cold when enveloped in the profound joy and hope that Christmas brings. And now, thanks to Mistletoe, we get to bring that feeling to people all year round."

The crowd cheered as Martin made his way back to Sadie and Nora.

"Thanks for that beautiful speech, Martin, but now let's get down to the good stuff." Mayor Evergreen strolled purposefully toward a huge red ribbon, its shimmering satin fabric elegantly stretched across the town square. Towering behind him stood an awe-inspiring forty-foot Christmas tree, its branches adorned with lights and colorful ornaments. In his hands, he grasped a pair of oversized ceremonial scissors, their blades glinting in the summer sunlight. With a warm, engaging smile, he addressed the eagerly awaiting crowd, "On the count of three, ready?" The air was thick with anticipation as he began the countdown. "One, two, three," echoed the crowd in a harmonious chorus.

With a decisive snip, the mayor cut through the ribbon, and in that instant, the Christmas tree erupted in a dazzling display of lights, illuminating the square and transforming it into a spectacular Christmas wonderland. The crowd's gasps of delight mingled with the soft jingle of holiday music, creating a moment of pure, enchanting beauty.

"Okay, then, I'm taking off to join my friends," Nora said.

"Home by eleven," Martin told her, and Nora gave him a mock salute.

When Nora left, Sadie reached into her pocket for the Santa hat Rosie had given her and pulled it onto her head. "I've been told it suits me. What do you think?"

Martin's laughter echoed across the square, but then he turned to her with a serious expression. "It certainly does, my love," he said, his voice deep and full of emotion, before capturing her lips in a kiss. "It certainly does."

I'm thrilled you've joined the adventure in the first book of the Kringle Cousin Romance series! If you enjoyed the journey, I'd be over the moon to hear your thoughts. A review or a star rating from you would be like a gift, letting others join in on the fun too. Your support is a treasure for authors like me.

About Janet Koops

A former librarian, Janet is a happily married empty-nester who writes full-time from her home just east of the Rocky Mountains. When she is not writing, she can typically be found hiking with her Alaskan Husky or working on a DIY project. Janet is a hopeless romantic who loves writing about complex women, their emotional journeys, and the healing power of love. Explore Janet's literary world further by visiting her official website. There, you'll find a comprehensive list of her published works. Additionally, become a part of Janet's reading community by subscribing to her newsletter, where you'll receive updates, insights, and exclusive content directly from the author.

Scan the QR code
or visit https://janetkoops.com

9 798986 552163